BOXSET - VAMPIRE ON THE RUN - BLOOD REBELLION - SEAL OF SOLOMON

Supernatural Intelligence Agency

NADINE TRAVERS

Fiction
Publication

CONTENTS

SEAL OF SOLOMON - LILANDRA REEVES ADVENTURE

SUPERNATURAL INTELLIGENCE AGENCY: WORLD - PREQUEL
VAMPIRE ON THE RUN
Every weekend
11AM to 3PM
OPEN
USA TODAY BESTSELLING AUTHOR
NADINE TRAVERS

License Note

Dépôt legal

Bibliothèque & Archives nationales du Québec 2020

Bibliothèque & Archives du Canada 2020

❧ Created with Vellum

BLURB

LIZBETH IS IN TROUBLE. DAMARIS KNOWS SHE'S DISCOVERED his plot to overthrow his brother Alto, the current head of the vampire family, and take his place. To keep her quiet and eliminate the threat, she poses, he's set her up and framed her for murder. Fleeing for her immortal life, she knows that every vampire blood-related to Alto is sacred and plotting against anyone who has consequences. Luckily, someone in the shifter community offers her shelter and to introduce her to someone who can help.

KANE, the half-demon, receives a message from a trusted source asking for help. His rescue mission goes up in flames when he realizes that not only is the damsel in distress a vampire but also his demon's destined mate.

WITH A MOUNTING amount of information and evidence coming their way, the paranormal community is on edge as the SIA and other factions work together to prevent a dark event that could change their world. Will they be able to stop it? Will Kane be able to protect his mate and have the life and happiness they deserve, or will the evil forces take over the community?

1. LIZBETH

I'VE BEEN FRAMED—THAT FUCKER DAMARIS HAS somehow placed the blame for the murder of one of his brother's bodyguards on me and I'm running for my life. I'm screwed and I know it. Alto is the head of our vampire faction and he won't let what he sees as a personal attack against him go unpunished. But how can I fight my maker's uncle and win against Damaris? I'm only a hundred years old and he is centuries old. Alto is going to believe his brother's lies over anything I have to say. As I said, I'm screwed.

My best bet is to stay in the neutral zone between worlds but as a vampire I need to hide during the day. Some of the hotels within the neutral zone provide that option. Luckily for me, one of the vampire factions owns a bar and dance club, while a shifter owns one of the hotels. Since they are part of the neutral zone, any paranormal species can rent a room or be inside the area and be safe. They have a special room for vampires in need, and that includes providing them with blood to drink.

Bran, Alto's son and Damaris's nephew, made me a vampire a hundred years ago. He loves tall, curvy women and

I was dying. I gained eternal life and a partner. At least that's what I thought I'd received for eternity, but having him reject me is my trump card in a way.

Since Bran hasn't drunk from me in more than fifty years, he can't locate me unless we're in close proximity to each other. Knowing Bran, I'm sure he's trying to lure another human into becoming his latest partner—over time I learned he's has a few different ones. I know when I first arrived after the transformation most of his previous partners wanted me dead. Bran only had eyes for me and when that faded, well, the bitches wanted to be my best friend. They wanted me to do to his new woman what they had done to me.

I didn't agree or answer them, not wanting to jump into a partnership, which gave me plenty of time to study and learn about the manor, history, and how the paranormal world worked. That knowledge helped me. I became invisible over time, as without Bran's protection I had a low status inside Alto's vampire family.

I look out the window—the city of Montreal is beautiful at night. I've rented a room for two days. I've never lost parts of my human side and Bran never understood why I still had a bank account in the human world, but today having that account saved me.

I hear a knock, look through the peephole, and see it's one of the hotel's employees. He's my contact and helped me to escape from Damaris. I open the door wide. "I wondered when you'd arrive."

He's brought some bottled blood, which he displays like he's holding a wine bottle. "Yeah, I had some difficulties. Some members of your clan were here. Don't worry though. We value secrecy and no one talked to them."

I'm thirsty, and I pour the blood into a glass. It isn't the best option, but for now, it will work. Human blood is excellent, but we need a lot more versus drinking another vampire's blood. One thing I didn't know at the time of my transformation is that it's possible to sustain yourself from the blood of other species but only if they are the same species as your mate.

"Bran was with them?"

The shifter liaison shakes his head. "No, he wasn't. From what I understand, it was his uncle."

"That fucker. Damaris was here?"

"Yes, I think that was his name. He didn't talk to me but to my boss. With the amount of money and gold you gave us, you don't need to worry you'll be betrayed."

Yes, another thing I value is gold. It's still a perfect way to trade security with other creatures. "Did he leave one of his goons at the hotel?"

"No, our security looked and didn't see anyone."

I sigh, maybe I'm free for now, but that also tells me I need to leave soon. "So your contact?"

He smiles at me. He's gorgeous for a dog, well, he's more of a werewolf. "He'll be at the Dragon Blood club tonight, here's a picture." He hands it over, all shifters are tall, but I think the guy in the photo is taller than average. "Yes, I know what you're thinking. Kane isn't a shifter. He's a half-demon. That's why he's so tall."

I look at the picture and him again. "A half-demon? I've never met one. I didn't realize there were any around here."

"There are a few of them. Not many though. Kane works for the Supernatural Intelligence Agency, and he's part of the Investigation Team. I told him your story and he was fascinated. Some of the other paranormal clans are noticing strange things happening in the community. He's in charge of collecting information."

"Can he be trusted?"

He chuckles. "You don't know much about half-demons, do you?"

"No. Sorry for my lack of education on the subject."

He grins at me. "Knowing you as I do, I'm surprised. There's one thing you need to know about half-demons. If they want to remain as half-demons, they have to stay on the right path. Until they find their mates at least."

"Why do they have to stay on the right path and why are their mates so important?"

"Inside him, each side wants to control the other. Half-demons usually make perfect soldiers in the human world since they are smaller than full demons and look human until they need to release their beast, which is different from what we do. I'm guessing he was hidden by his human mother and raised without any influence from his demon father. He needs to find his mate to keep in control of his beast."

That was interesting. "So, he's luckier than others but he could still fail unless he finds his mate?"

"Look, I know you're a hundred years old but he's got a century on you. If anyone has an influence on our world, it's him. He's saved my life countless times in the past and brought me here where I found a pack again and gained some stability in my life."

I look at him. "That's why you're helping me?"

"In a way. I've got my reasons, but I'll tell you this much. I've also been framed in the past, and he was the one that brought down the bad guys and kept me alive in the process. So, yes, I believe in him, and he believes your story. One thing though, you can't lie to him. Your aura changes when you lie, and he will know. You'll understand when you meet him."

I nod at him.

"I'll bring you clothes that are more suitable for a night-club. Don't thank me, you'll be in good hands with Kane, but until then, stay here. That gives you two hours to prepare, and I'll take you there. I can't go inside as I'm banned from that place. You need to find the tallest man at the bar, that will be him."

With that he leaves me to prepare, and I need to eat too. That way I won't be tempted to find someone to satisfy my thirst.

2. KANE

I CHOSE THIS CLUB BECAUSE I KNEW ALEX WAS banned from it. I don't want him to mingle with different species just yet—he needs the stability of the pack until he finds his mate. Not that I'm surprised Alex called me to help someone. What does surprise me is that it's to help a vampire. Alex despises vampires, but when he told me her story, I was interested.

According to him, she was framed because she saw something that could interest the Investigation Team, which it does. Something is happening inside the paranormal community and the more information we get as to what is going on, the better.

I'm at my usual spot and it's pretty easy to notice me with my height. The DJ inside the club is insane. I look around, several different species are mixing together and talking or doing other things. I'm in the neutral zone, which means it's part of the government's territory. Vampires tend to own clubs like this, since it's more their lifestyle and they can access blood from humans and vampires from other clans.

One of Katy Perry's songs is playing and the dance floor is

crowded. The variety of species here tonight is huge. I can see a vampire, a werewolf, witches, faes, another shifter, another half-demon and also humans. Most of them don't know about us, but some are well aware and want to be part of it. My phone buzzes and I pull it out to see a text from Alex.

SHE'S INSIDE.

All my senses become alert and the need to find her is strong. I stand to make it easier for her to spot me. A faint smell of lavender hits my nose and I inhale deeply. Flowers have never attracted me, they remind me of a lot of things, but for the first time something sparks inside me. I spot her. She's tall for a woman, but with lush curves that make me drool on the spot. She's got dark blond hair—she's gorgeous.

She belongs to us! I jolt, surprised. Since when does my beast talk to me in my head?

"Are you Kane?"

I smile at her. I want to run my hand over her body to discover her curves. "I am, and you're Lizbeth, the vampire in trouble."

She looks around. I can tell she's nervous as she takes a deep breath. "Yes, but don't say things like that here. Goons are everywhere."

I finished my drink and pay the bartender before taking her hand. I suspected something when I saw her, but now I've touched her I know. She's my mate, my fated one. The beast wants out, to play and to claim. I need to control him, now isn't the time. My dick is hard as stone. Fuck, I need to get us out of here and fast.

I hope Alex is waiting for us in his car near the back entrance like we discussed. I put my hand on her back to show her the way.

"Where are we going?"

"We need to leave, staying here will attract too much attention and I suspect you don't need that right now."

She doesn't fight and follows me. I keep a tight hold of her hand as a lot of people are in the club tonight, but before we reach the exit I hear my name being called.

"Kane!"

Shit not now. Both of us turn. "Mel. What are you doing here?" I keep my mate close to me and put my arms around her waist to show Mel she belongs to me. I thought she would fight it, but she goes along with me, relaxing in my embrace.

"Kane, I didn't think I'd ever see you with a bloodsucker." Mel is a human, but she knows about the paranormal community and she loves it. I think she hopes to find a partner with one of us.

"Don't start." I bring my mate closer to me. She puts her hand on my chest. Fuck, now my brain is overloaded.

"Well, now you know he's with me, so get lost," Lizbeth says narrowing her eyes at Mel.

I smile inside, mates are possessive, and I know by their reputation vampires are the worst.

When Mel doesn't leave my mate puts her hand under my t-shirt and claws my skin. *Ah fuck, that's a major turn-on.* "Seriously, you need to leave. Now."

Before I fully register her words, she grabs the back of my neck and claims my lips. It's electric. My demon takes control of the kiss. It's pure carnage to my senses. She doesn't give me access inside her mouth but I push it, I badly need to taste her.

She finally grants me access, and I take the opportunity to completely possess her mouth. Her curves meld into my body, but I need more. I want to be inside her, my dick demands it, and so do I. I grab the back of her head which makes it impossible for her to move. I growl inside her mouth as she jumps and puts her legs around my waist.

I can smell her—she's wet for me. I push her against the wall knowing everyone can see us, but I don't fucking care. I want everyone to know she belongs to me. I look in her eyes. They are red and full of desire and something else I can't put my finger on. Her fangs are showing and I know what she needs but if she does it right now, I'll shred our clothing and claim her in front of everyone.

"What do you think about taking this somewhere else?"

She hisses at my request. "I need a taste. To claim."

It seems she has issues controlling her instincts which is something she'll learn in time.

"Hey! Take that somewhere else. You know the rules."

I look over my shoulder as the bartender looks at me. "Yes, sir, I will. Don't worry."

He nods and continues to work.

I gently lower her to her feet. "We need to go, there's a car waiting for us. I'm taking you back to my place until we can sort your situation out."

She follows me without resistance, but I know she wants more and so do I.

3. LIZBETH

AH, FUCK, WHAT JUST HAPPENED? NOT ONLY WAS I in a club where some of Alto's family could be, but I'd jumped the half-demon that was supposed to be protecting me. I'm losing my mind.

"Don't worry, everyone in the club has seen more than we showed them."

"Great, so now I'm entertainment for you and the club?"

He stops in his tracks and grabs my jaw in his big hands. "You're my mate, and you know that. You can't deny it, and I don't want to deny it either."

I look at him. He's good looking, with his tall, muscular frame, short brown hair, and yellow eyes. I need to control myself. *Fuck,* I want to jump him again. I need more. I need his blood.

"Alex is waiting for us. We'll have more time to talk and get to know each other at my place. It's bulletproof and nobody would dare enter my domain." He pushes me outside the club, and I recognize Alex's car.

Kane makes me hop in before sitting beside me in the

back of the vehicle. "Alex, take us to my hideout. You know where it is."

Alex looks at Kane like he's lost his mind. "You're sure?"

Kane passes his hand through his hair and sighs. "Yes, do it."

Alex smiles and shakes his head but doesn't say anything else. We head to an area I'm unfamiliar with and a couple of minutes later we arrive at a gate. Kane hops out and punches in a code. The gate opens, and he jumps back in the car before we head up the drive. Once the car stops again, I get out and wait while Kane talks to Alex. I'm pretty sure Alex is teasing him from the big grin on his face.

I try to control myself. I know deep down Kane is the one for me. I may have drunk before going to the club, but now my thirst is back. I should have until tomorrow after the sun is down before I need to drink again, but I know this need is something else. For now, I don't have a choice but to wait and I wonder if he feels the same. I look around and see we are still in the neutral zone. "You live here?"

His eyes intense gaze at me. "Yes, but it's also designed as a safe house. It's totally secure. We'll stay here for the time being. After that, we'll see."

Alex goes to the back of the car and grabs some luggage that isn't mine. The only bag I have is my backpack.

"Lizbeth, here, we got you some stuff you may need and some blood for you to drink. Once it's gone Kane will help you to find more blood."

I nod, stunned. Nobody has ever done anything like this for me, let alone the fact it's a shifter helping a vampire. I give him a big hug. "Thank you so much." I don't know what else to say.

I grab the bag and follow Kane inside. I don't know what my future holds, but for now I know I can rely on him. He opens the door and gestures for me to enter first and I smirk at him as I enter. The notion you have to invite a vampire inside is wrong and comes from the movies. It's dark inside, I can't see a lot of windows, but the place has the feel of a cottage. He turns on the light—I don't need it to see, but maybe he does, although I suspect he doesn't.

"Come, I'll show you to your room."

I follow him even though I'm not tired. Yes, during the day I need to sleep but not at night. He opens a door, and I enter a comfortable room. "This room doesn't have any windows, which will be better for you. The sun will be up in a couple of hours. Do you need to drink before then or are you good?"

"No, I not. I should be fine, and I don't understand why I'm not. I know Alex put blood inside my luggage, but I don't feel like drinking it. I'm..."

I'm not able to finish my sentence before Kane kisses me—it's hard, possessive, and full of lust. I'm not able to control myself, and I encircle his waist with my legs, needing to feel all of him.

He backs me against the wall and pushes against me allowing me to feel how hard and big his dick is. "You know what this means. Tell me you feel the same."

How can I answer him? I know from watching others what is happening. "I don't know."

He puts his hand on my butt and squeezes it hard. I hiss, and he takes advantage of it to kiss me more deeply. I know my fangs and claws are out. I forget about the blood inside the luggage—all I want is to drink from him, all of him.

He stops the kiss and we're both breathless. I don't need to air to survive, but I never stopped the physical action of breathing after been turned into a vampire.

"Do I have to say it? You're thirsty, but you don't want the blood Alex gave you. You're craving mine and mine alone."

"I need vampire blood to survive. Other blood isn't strong enough."

He smiles at me and puts his nose in the base of my neck. "The reason you want my blood is because I'm your mate and your body knows it. From now on you will only drink from me and me alone."

I pass my tongue over my lips. I'm drooling for his taste, I crave it. I put my hand under his shirt and scratch him. I know I've drawn blood, I can smell it. It's like a drug and I begin to move my hips harder against him. I want him wild before I drink and I need him deep inside me to do so.

He hisses and smiles. "You're craving, and I know what you need."

With that said, he lets me go and strips in front of me. Sex with Bran was ordinary and fun, but what I feel now is consuming me. If he doesn't possess me soon, I will die. If I don't drink from him, I will die.

His muscles are well defined and he grins as he catches me staring at his chest before my eyes move lower. "Like what are you see?"

I knew he would be big everywhere. His dick is huge. I want it in my mouth, in my pussy, and in my ass. I'm guessing half-demons have a lot of stamina, similar to a shifter or vampire, which gives us about three hours before I need to sleep. I intend to satisfy my thirst and claim my mate in the process.

4. KANE

AH, FUCK! I'D NEVER ONCE CONSIDERED MY MATE WOULD be a vampire. I need to pay Alex back double for this. My beast wants out too; he wants to mark her the same way I do.

Lizbeth strips while I wait and watch. Her skin is white and smooth. She's not wearing a bra and it's obvious her tits are real and ready for me. I'm drooling and I stroke my dick in reaction to having just had a private strip show. She hisses in reaction.

"Don't stop, continue. I want you naked."

She removes her pants and panties at the same time. I knew when vampires are transformed, they lost their body hair so I'm not surprised her pussy is bare to my touch. Her fangs are visible once more, her needs apparent. I've never had a vampire drink from me and this will be a first. Usually, they need strong blood to survive, which is why they drink from other vampires or from their mates even if they aren't a vampire. They need sex, but drinking their mate's blood is the link that bonds them. For us half-demons, bonding occurs with the need to impregnate our mate along with our beast's need to bite his mate.

Among pure demon clans, the concept of a mate doesn't exist. The idea of having a mate evolved when demons started breeding with human females to have half-demon children. It's those children that have the need to mate. I look at her as she chews on her bottom lip which has me on the verge of coming.

"You know what that means?" she asks me.

I smile and stroke her cheek before taking her jaw between my hands. "Yes, I know."

I claim her lips. I want our joining to be slow and emotional, but as soon as I touch her lips, the other side takes control. It's carnage, even for her. She puts her arms around my neck, and I grab her ass. She responds by wrapping her legs around me again. I knew it would be like this—hot and demanding. Now I'm able to feel all of her. She pulls back from the kiss and hisses.

"Tell me you want it, my beautiful vampire. I need to hear you say it."

She moves against me. I know she's having trouble speaking, but I need to hear it anyway. I put her on the bed without releasing her, holding her tight against me. "Tell me!" I growl at her. My beast is there with us; he needs to hear it.

"Yes. Oh, god! Please."

I smile and stroke my nose against her neck. She scratches my back and once more I can feel blood welling there. I don't mind, half-demons heal fast and we have a high pain threshold.

"Tell us!" I capture her face, forcing her to look at me. Her eyes are red; her teeth are out. The signs of the mating fever are obvious, but I still need to hear it before I claim her.

"Are you sure?" I know my voice is altered because of the beast.

"Yes, I'm yours."

With that, I take my dick in my hand, guiding it to her

entrance before pushing inside. "Ah, fuck, you're tight." I look in her eyes needing to see her pleasure. I know she's able to take me since she's my mate, but part of me requires the knowledge she knows what's happening.

Her mouth is open, and I can see the pleasure on her face.

Lizbeth looks at me. "This is what they mean when they say you claim your mate?"

I smile. "Yes, I need to claim you. You ready?" I'm as far inside her as it's possible to be. She nods and I move my hips slowly to begin with as I don't want to hurt her.

"More!" She grabs my ass, pulling me tighter as I thrust inside her.

I grin, happy to give her more. I wanted to go slow, to take my time, and I wanted it to last until forever but she's too responsive, and it makes me wild. *My mate.* After two hundred years I've found her. She's perfect for me. Her fangs grab my attention again. "Don't worry. You will have your fill before sunrise." My demon's fangs are there, too. That's the way we claim our mate.

She scrapes her fangs over my neck where it meets my shoulder joint. "I need to claim you," she replies.

I understand her need because I'm in the same state. I gradually increase my tempo and she screams louder. I kiss her on her neck in the same place. The temptation to bite her is powerful. "Tell me you're mine, now!" I grab her head and make her look at me. As soon as I see the look on her face I know I'm not going to be able to last. She licks her lips, I groan with the temptation. She's a fucking gorgeous temptress. She arches against me and I can tell it's a deliberate move to make me lose control.

My movements are chaotic now as I lose all finesse. "Tell us!"

Usually, a vampire doesn't breathe, but she does and her

chest is moving up and down as she pants. She's kept part of herself from before her transformation, which I like, a lot.

"Claim me like I'm going to claim you."

Her words are a trigger and I lose control. I push deep inside Lizbeth and bite hard on her neck.

She screams at my invasion but also my claim. She licks at the same spot on my neck again and scratches her claws into my back. I increase the rhythm of my thrusts.

"Yes!" She screams, and bites down hard, harder than I thought she would.

5. LIZBETH

I BITE HIM, HARDER THAN I'D EVER BITTEN SOMEONE before. He has bitten my neck as well. The mating is done.

"Arg! Your pussy is gripping me like a vice."

I can't talk anymore. I can only feel Kane claiming me as I claim him and it's unlike anything I've ever experienced. His fangs finally let go, and he licks the bite. His saliva leaves a mark on my neck, a way to show the world I belong to him.

"I'm coming!" I release his neck and lick his wound and he kisses me hard. His movements inside me are strong and fast. I love it; my body needs more. He grabs my tits and plays with my nipples, pinching them. I lose track of everything. I'm on fire with desire. I need to release it.

"Come for me!" he growls.

He bites one of my nipples, and that's all it takes. "Kane!" I scream.

I come like I never have before, even when I was human. I know he is close to his release so I squeeze his cock harder and he yells. The sound he makes is somewhere between human and demonic. He comes hard. I don't know much about half-demons, but one thing I do know is that they can only impregnate their mates and the idea of having his baby doesn't scare me as much as I thought it would.

"Ah fuck!" He moves aside but grabs me in his arms.

"I didn't think it would be that intense," I tell him.

He laughs. "Yes, I agree. The night is not finished, but you need to sleep, which is why we're here. You're young for a vampire, and I know you need to sleep all day, unlike older ones."

True, the older we become as a vampire the less sleep we need but we still need to stay inside during daylight because the sun is fatal for us. "I think you know more than you want to share," I say to him.

He runs his hand over my back stroking it slowly. "Maybe. What did Alex tell you about me?"

"Not a lot, only you're someone that helps people in my situation and you keep them safe. He told me that you saved his life in the past and that's the reason he helped me in return. He knew I wasn't lying when I told him my story."

He doesn't answer right away. "True, but I do that for other reasons. I'm part of the SIA Investigation Team. We investigate weird and unusual things inside the paranormal community but also any crimes that aren't immediately solved by the individual factions."

I look at him but don't anything. I don't know much about the extended paranormal community, only the faction that became my family when I was transformed. "I don't know much outside the vampire world."

He kisses me on my lips briefly. "Well, not all factions want to play together nicely, which is why the Supernatural Intelligence Agency exists. I'm part of the Investigation Team, but we have other departments as well depending on the case. We have a warrior witch as part of the special operations team, but we also have librarians who work with us."

"That means you work for the government with different kinds of species?"

"Yes, we try to get along. Sometimes it's difficult but time usually helps us to sort out our differences."

I wonder what it's like to work with others. It's been almost a hundred years since I left my blood family. I had no idea that different species interacted in that way. The more he talks, the more I want to know. "So you know witches and werewolves?"

He smiles at me. "Yes and more. We have all the older breeds, like the faes, witches, werewolves and other kinds of shifters, as well as vampires, telepaths, empaths, and that's doesn't include half-breeds like me."

"Wow, I never knew. Alto's clan is very secretive. Only a few are transformed for their blood. Alto's son wants to find his mate, but he's not serious yet so he transforms a girl he's in lust with and after a few years he dumps her for someone new."

He kisses me on my forehead. We are still naked and talking about our pasts. It should be uncomfortable but it isn't. "How was life there?"

I look in his eyes. "Great at first, but after a while not so much." He takes my hand and keeps silent until I'm ready to talk. "I thought I was in love. Bran is a gorgeous man and I was young. I'd just turned twenty-one, and he was the first man to look at me and desire me and he captivated me. I guess if he hadn't done what he did, I wouldn't be here with you now. In a way, I owe him."

He smiles at me. "True, but fate always finds a way to the right path. I'm sorry he did what he did, but at the same time I'm not."

"I feel the same now, but I didn't feel like that at the beginning. The first few years were great. Bran treated me right. I had a high rank within the family since I was Bran's favorite, but I should have known better—that it doesn't last. I thought they were my friends. When he stopped his adventure with me, they turned away and wouldn't talk to me. I was at the top, yet the minute he took another one, I lost any status I had within the family. They didn't physically hurt me, but it did hurt to begin with, and after a while I was left alone which was a blessing. I was able to walk around the manor and found some interesting places that everyone had forgotten about over time."

He pulls me back on his chest. "Now you're with me for eternity. I'm two hundred years old. I'm glad I found you, but at the same time, I'm not happy with the way you were treated. After this is finished, we will have the rest of our lives together, but we need to take care of your situation first. The way I see it, it's not good. I have some of my team investigating Alto's family, and we'll see what they come up with. For now, we'll stay here and keep a low profile until we catch or reveal your enemy."

I kiss his defined chest. I loved a man's abs when I was human, and now it's worse. I can feel in my body the time to sleep is almost here. I look at him and gently kiss him again. "Thanks for being there and meeting with me even though you didn't know I was your mate."

He kisses me on my head as darkness claims me and I sleep.

6. DAMARIS

"YOU'RE A FUCKING FOOL. WE NEED TO FIND Lizbeth. I want a result."

"But Lizbeth has disappeared." One of my human goons stands before me. He wants to be a vampire, and I agreed to change him. Before I do though he needs to show me he's worthy of being part of my clan.

"You will need to find a way. Find Tom. He's a cop and part of my crew. With his help, you should be able to find her."

That bitch Bran transformed into a vampire could jeopardize everything. We need this clan to be great again. I'm the head vampire's only brother, but when Alto had a son my chance to be on top was gone. By birth leadership will go to him. That young one without any common sense. He wants to find love, his mate. That doesn't exist.

We fuck and breed or transform those that are worth it and the rest is futile. I don't believe my brother agrees with what Bran does, or gave him the green light with his activities but he won't stop him either. Our clan is strong but it needs to be stronger. By leaving and forming a new clan we can avoid the politics and hierarchies that currently exist. I need that.

"Master?" Someone enters my bedroom and I look up to see another of my loyal humans. "We know where she is but we can't get to her." He looks at the floor.

Rage increases inside me. "Why?" I scream at him.

"She's with that half-demon, the one that works for the SIA Investigation Team."

I freeze on the spot at his reply. That fucking bastard. I grab the nearest object and throw it at the wall. "That fucker. I need both of them gone. You know what you have to do. They need to die."

He doesn't say anything else and leaves me alone.

That half-demon has given me a lot of headaches in the past, that fucker. He's always there helping the weaker ones. He will pay because now he has something I desperately need and in the process I can kill two birds with one stone. *Yes, that's the right place to start*. We need her to be taken out with him. With that decided, I head to bed. I'm old, but I still need a couple of hours in the darkness.

I lay on the bed and let sleep claim me. Tomorrow night my goons—and I hope for their sakes they do—will have more information we can use to create a plan to kill them both.

7. KANE

MY LIFE HAS CHANGED IN JUST A COUPLE OF HOURS. I'll need to change my routine since my mate is a night owl. She molds herself to me in her sleep. She's probably cold since she's a vampire, but I've got plenty of heat to give her.

I've had a few misconceptions about vampires. I knew they sleep during the day, but I thought they were stiff and didn't move, which isn't the case. She's like a human, tossing and turning and sighing in her sleep. I wonder what a vampire dreams about. I need to sleep to be awake during the night, but since I have the chance to observe her without her knowledge, I take it.

I move so we're facing each other and reach out to stroke Lizbeth's hair. The strands are smooth, almost like velvet. I touch her cheek, and it's soft and smooth like a baby. Her skin feels cold, but that's normal for a vampire.

Her lips are red and bring sinful thoughts to my head. The mating is done, which puts my beast more under my control than it's used to, but that's OK. She moans in her sleep, and I wonder again what she's dreaming about. Between moans, I hear her whisper my name. My dick stirs, now hard and wanting to play. I know she needs more sleep as it's still light outside, but I can't resist her.

I turn her so her back is against my chest and pinch her nipples again. I love her gorgeous tits, they fit perfectly in my hands. She moans deeper and starts moving against my dick. I hiss at her movement. I don't know if she's awake or dreaming about something hot and steamy. I kiss her shoulder where I marked her—the mark tells every paranormal creature she's off-limits and belongs to me. I have the same mark on the side of my neck, which says the same thing —that I belong to her.

I nip her skin as my hand continues exploring. I stroke her belly and hips, and moving lower my fingers touch her center. She moans and says my name in the process. *Fuck.* I want her fully awake, but this will do, and I know she's going to wake soon.

I open her legs a little and play with her clit. She's ready for me—wet and hot. I don't know much about how mating works for a vampire but for us half-demons, we need to impregnate our mate. I wonder if vampires can have children, but since she's my fated mate, I guess she can.

"Oh, god!"

I nip hard on her shoulder, drawing a bit of blood but not too much, just enough for a taste. I continue my exploration of her center wishing I could taste her. I need her taste in my mouth and to make her come in the process. My beast and I are drooling at the idea.

"Oh, Kane, don't stop."

I chuckle against her shoulder. "Never. Is my sleeping beauty finally awake?"

She smiles. "Not yet, she needs more of that."

"Challenge accepted."

I turn her on her back, and claim what I'm drooling over and fantasizing about. I kiss her belly, before moving further down and open her legs more and put them over my shoulders. My demon's fangs are out too and I use them to scratch the skin close to her center—her flesh is tender and tastes delicious.

"Oh, god, don't stop!" she screams.

I chuckle against her pussy and continue my exploration with my tongue. I put one finger inside her as I continue to suck her clit. She makes noises that make me harder just hearing them.

"I'm so close, Kane," she screams at me.

I continue teasing her. Her claws dig into my biceps as I reach up and enclose her tit with my hand, pinching her nipple with the same rhythm as I'm sucking her clit. I feel it now and know she's there.

"Kane!" She screams as she comes. She lies on the bed, breathless before turning her head to look at me. "You're ruining me."

I laugh at her words. "That goes both ways, just to let you know."

She smiles. "Now it's my turn. I've heard you half-demons have a lot of stamina."

I grin at her. "You heard correctly."

She gets a wicked smile on her face. "I need to test it."

She moves over my dick, which hurts with how hard it is. She licks it slowly, testing my sensitivity I guess. I hiss. I want to tell her to continue and to stop torturing me at the same time. "Oh, god!" I let myself be surrounded by the feeling of her mouth on me. Having a vampire for a mate is the best. She takes me fully in her mouth and deep into her throat. My beast wants to come out and play. I know my voice is growling and deep, partly because of my beast.

She lets go of my dick with a pop. "I think someone wants to play."

I chuckle at her statement; he wants more. I take control

and put her on all fours and keep her there. She tries to fight me, but without success. Vampires are strong, but half-demons are stronger. "Let me claim you the way I want. My cock wants to be inside you so bad, and I can't wait until tonight."

She looks at me over her shoulder, her fangs are out, and her crystal blue eyes are red with desire. "I need you, all of you."

I smile, from what I know about vampires, they need to drink a lot when they mate to make the bond stronger. The stronger that bond gets, the more they can live for eternity until one of them is dead.

I lift her slightly, align my dick with her center, and enter her swiftly. My need to dominate her completely is almost overwhelming.

"Oh, god!"

I kiss her back up to her neck and play with her nipples at the same time, pinching them, hurting them a little. I kiss where I've marked her. "No, not god, only a half-demon that is head over heels for you," I growl, needing to hear the words from her.

"Yes, please." I bite her. "More, harder!"

"As you wish!" I whisper to her.

8. LIZBETH

I ASK HIM FOR HARDER, AND I NEED IT. MY BODY doesn't belong to me any longer and I'm just a puppet in his arms.

"Tell me you're mine!"

I'm not usually turned on by a male's display of possessiveness, but with him, it's different. "Yes, I'm yours, all of me." I need to claim, but I need to drink also. Even though I drank from him a couple of hours ago, I need more. That's the mating fever for a vampire.

He pumps harder inside me, but I need to taste his blood. With the position I'm in I can't reach his neck. He lets me go, probably sensing there's something I want. I push against him until he's sitting against the bedhead and straddle him so we're facing each other. Leaning forward, I kiss him at the same time I take his cock inside me again.

He hisses at my torture. I look at him, holding his gaze as I lick my lips. I know that affects him from the way he grabs my hips and pulls me hard against him. I want to claim his blood again, the need to mark him is overwhelming me. He makes me wild with need and it's worse since he's my mate.

"Your blood smells so sweet; I need to drink it."

He chuckles and smiles at me. "Do it. I'm the only one that will give you blood for the rest of eternity."

I smile, loving his possessiveness. I don't know the normal life span of a half-demon, but I'm guessing that mating and exchanging blood gives him an extension of life to match mine. I lick the skin between his neck and shoulder. The vein in the neck is one place we can tap, the other is on the inside of his legs. He hisses at my licking, but without warning, I bite him as sensually as I can. He's hard inside me, but now it's worse and I can feel him getting harder and bigger. I keep my prize under my fangs and drink from him, he shouts and comes. Without delay he tilts his head and his fangs sink into my neck, which triggers my own orgasm. Having sex with another paranormal creature is amazing but when that paranormal creature is your mate, the pleasure increases by a thousand.

I scream against his neck but continue to tap his vein for his blood. When I'm satisfied, and we've had our release, I release his neck and lick his wound.

He mirrors my actions. "Ah fuck, I didn't think finding my mate would have me wanting to have sex all the time."

He laughs softly. "Maybe, but that doesn't mean I don't love it."

I lift myself from him and lie on top of the bed.

He joins me, lying on his side and propping his head in his hand.

"So, what happens now?"

"And just like that it's back to reality."

I chuckle. "Maybe, but I don't like that people want to eliminate me."

He growls and tightens his hold on me. "I'm waiting for information from the team and Alex. Something nasty is starting to circulate inside the remote circles."

I push myself up on my elbow. "Like what?"

He looks at me, and I'm not reassured by his expression. "We can only speculate at the moment, but with what Alex has brought me, along with your problems, things are starting to take form and make a bit more sense. We thought this was something to do with the shifters, but now we know vampires are also implicated it adds up to a big problem. We know from fact and history that both factions have a serious feud happening between them, but if they are working together for something bigger than themselves, it also means individuals could infiltrate other factions in some way."

I look at him. "I know Damaris was talking about a group, but I thought it was other vampires. I agree. Werewolves in particular have been feuding with vampires for a millennium which makes no sense."

He runs his hand over my back and kisses my forehead. "Don't worry. I won't let them take you."

"You said the team is helping, and so is Alex. Why are you not working the case?"

He grabs my head and looks into my eyes. "I'm personally involved now. You being my mate will make me biased, and my priority is to keep you alive no matter the cost. I'll let my boss know I'm still on the case but only as your protection. The rest of the investigation will be taken over by a couple of friends of mine. Don't worry, they are the best."

I go over in my mind everything we know so far. I understand now why he wants me to disappear. "Do you think Damaris wants to rule over Alto's family?"

"That could be the case. Maybe Damaris was promised something he could never otherwise have."

"True, even if he is Alto's brother, he can never rule since Alto has a son that will become leader after he becomes dust. I knew he was desperate for power, but I didn't think he would go against his blood family."

He gently strokes my hair. "Maybe, but that also means he's got followers. I doubt he's working alone. We're starting to think that maybe they're forming another faction, although we don't know for sure. The only things we know so far are from whispers inside the community. It was enough to concern us, and with the addition of your story, my division in the SIA couldn't ignore it."

I wish I had more information for him, for us. "I'm happy I survived and found you at the end. I don't know what our future holds but that doesn't mean I don't want to live life one hundred percent. Now more than ever."

He kisses my head and tightens his hold on me and I melt into his embrace. I've been lucky so far but how long will that luck last? I know them, and Damaris in particular. He wants power above all else and I'm an obstacle in his path.

"Don't worry you're not alone anymore. You've got me, the team, and Alex's group. They also want to help in the investigation. The alpha wants them exposed, if not killed. I think most of us want peace, but it seems others want something that brings destruction to gain power."

He's right. We need to stop them, the balance in the community is in jeopardy. I hope this little revolt is small, and we can stop it before it becomes too big.

9. KANE

NIGHT IS FALLING, AND SHE'S SO IMPATIENT I CAN feel vibrating it in the air around us. Our bond is growing stronger and stronger. That also means we will soon be able to hear each other's thoughts and know where each other is all the time. The blood gives us that power. I smile as I watch her. "Stop pacing!" She turns, and I can see the worry on her face. It's going to be a long night if she doesn't settle.

"We can't stay here like this. I'm going crazy. We need to do something."

I force her to stop pacing and look at her. "Worrying won't solve anything, we need a plan, but to do that we need more information." I know mates can't kill each other, but the look in her eyes tells me she's not happy with my words.

"We need to do something now."

"My little warrior, we will but now is not the time." My phone vibrates inside my pants pocket and I pull it out and answer it. "Yes, Kane here."

"It's me, Alex. We've found some information. The alpha wants both of you back at the hotel. It's big, man. I'm not sure we have all the intel, but maybe your team has found something as well."

I sigh. I knew in my gut it wasn't something small that was going on within the community. I should've had more faith in myself and my instincts. "We're on our way. Be there in thirty minutes. Security?"

"At the maximum, we've even got witches with us. That how big this is."

I end the call. "Fuck!"

She grabs my arm. "What?"

"Shit! We need to head back to the hotel. Alex and his pack have news. Not only that, the witches are there too."

Her eyes widen. We work in absolute harmony inside the community within the neutral zone which brings humans and other paranormal species together, but anything regarding trading, security, and other factional things are generally kept within the factions. While they will work with each other, it's more businesslike than personal. If the witches are involved, it's because this is bigger than us.

I text my team at the agency and they reply saying Ross and Kass will be there also. "This is bad. Every group from our agency will be there. Get ready. We need to head to the hotel."

She nods but doesn't say much, we know if other factions are starting to meld and come together, it isn't good. It could lead to a civil war inside the community against humans.

I'm amazed at the speed a vampire in a rush can do things and let out a laugh.

"What?"

I go to her and quickly kiss her lips. "Well, I knew vampires could move fast, I just didn't realize how fast."

She smiles. "Well lucky for you, you'll never have to wait for your woman to be ready. Which could make others jealous."

I laugh. "Maybe the future will tell us." I slap her butt, and we leave the house. Once we're in my SUV, I head directly to the hotel.

"What?" she asks when she notices I'm constantly checking my mirrors.

"We're being followed." I noticed the black car leaving the same time we did. I've tried to create some distance between us but without any success. "Recognize the car?"

She looks back. "Ah fuck, that's Stan's car, and I can see John as well."

I wished I was wrong. "Who are they?"

She chews her bottom lips. "No one good. They are Damaris's right-hand men. They are his top human goons for doing things for him."

I increase my speed trying to lose them. It's late, but a lot of people are still up in downtown Montreal. We need to get closer to the Old Port, which is part of the neutral zone.

"Are you able to lose them?"

I sigh. "Doing my best. Hold on." I grab my phone and hit speed dial. "Greg!"

"I'm here, mate. What can I do?"

She looks at me puzzled, wondering what I'm up to then I see understanding in her eyes as I focus back on Greg. "I need you to hack the lights around my position."

I hear a chair moving and tapping on a keyboard. "What are you close to and where are you heading?"

I give him the information. "You need to do it fast. They're getting closer. You're my eyes now, find me the fastest way out of here."

"I'm on it. OK, turn right, now."

I shift the car and head down a small street that seems empty.

"I'll try to hack into their cell phones and turn them off.

They seem to be tracking you somehow. Left." I do what he tells me.

"Tracking?" It's taking longer than it should to lose them.

"Left again, you're close. I advised the hotel that you're coming, but you're being chased. They've hacked your GPS system."

"Shit! Come on, Greg!" I hear him playing on his keyboard.

"Right and right after that. I'll try something. I need to shut the GPS down, if not, they'll know where you are."

I quickly look at Lizbeth, and she's looking out the rear window again. "Ah fuck, he's got a gun."

"Greg, we're running out of time."

"Left and left, enter that small place and hide behind the trees. I'm turning it off."

I do what he says and stop the car, but I keep my hand on the key in case I need to restart fast and move again. A couple of seconds later they pass us, and we wait a couple more minutes. A minute has never felt so long.

"You're clear, mate. Alex is waiting for you. I'd ditch the car. I don't know how long I can keep them out. Whoever hacked the system is good, really good."

"Are we far from the hotel?"

"No, a couple of blocks. It would probably be quicker for you to go on foot anyway because of the traffic and you don't have tracking devices on you."

I signal to Lizbeth to get out of the car.

"Keep your phone on. I'll follow you on the CCTV cameras just in case they reappear."

"Thanks, man. Is the team ready?"

"We are. Call us when you need us."

"I will, don't worry." I end the call. "Come. We need to get to the hotel fast. We'll use the back entrance. I'm pretty sure they've got someone on the front."

She nods at me, and we start walking. I put in my earpiece in case Greg calls me. When we reach the hotel I knock at the door and a small window opens and we see Alex.

He opens the door. "Come, we've got news. Where's your car?"

"Long story. It'll be easier if we tell everyone at once. I need you to find me a new car, I had to ditch mine for now."

Alex nods and shows us the way. We enter a large conference room, and it's filled with people looking at us.

I look at her. "Don't worry, love, nothing will happen to you." I push her inside and close the door.

10. LIZBETH

I'VE NEVER SEEN SO MANY PEOPLE IN ONE PLACE. Kane introduces me to Ross and Kass, the heads of his group. I sit on a chair, and Kane stands behind me. Ross and Kass sit on either side of me, Alex and his group sit at one end, and the witches are in opposite us.

"All of us know part of what is going on, and I'll tell you what I know and why Lizbeth is part of it." Everyone nods at Kane's statement and he tells them how Alex called him about a rescue situation with a vampire that saw something she shouldn't have. "I don't know all the details, Lizbeth can tell you more. I can tell you they badly want her, enough to target an agent from the agency. They followed us here with the intent to capture or kill us. It sure wasn't an invitation to a tea party."

I smile at his words.

"Can you tell us more, Lizbeth?"

I look at one of the witches and recognize her from the club where I first met Kane. "Sure, but I want to know more about all of you first. Why are the witches involved in this?"

The three witches look at each other, the older one, at

least she seems older than the others, rises from her chair. "We have some information. We are part of the witches' government, meaning that while each coven has its own internal affairs, we oversee all of them. I'm Gwen Kahnis, and I was what you'd call a lone witch for a long time. Other covens have started talking about people or artifacts that have gone missing or have been stolen. That's a first. The only way that could happen is if it was someone on the inside. One thing's for sure, some of the warrior witch covens have started to get calls from hidden artifacts which aren't supposed to be found."

"Calls?"

She sighs. "Well, one way of explaining it is that some of us have had distinct impressions. The warrior witches can fight with or without a weapon, but they also get callings from artifacts that could be in the wrong hands. The calling doesn't happen like this. Lately they don't have the time to stop and heal between fights, which is causing our healers to have to work overtime as well."

"I see. What I can tell you is this..." I tell them my story, about Alto and his son Bran but mostly about his blood brother Damaris and the murder of Alto's security guard.

"Well, this is odd. Usually, blood is more important than anything with vampires."

"True, but in his case, he can't be the head of the faction since Alto has a son with his human mate. Automatically, leadership will go to Bran directly without a fight or debate within the clan. I think Damaris badly wants to be in charge and has probably been promising power to those who help him which he can't have until Bran is killed. Alto still has his human mate with him. She lives on his blood for now. That doesn't mean she couldn't have another child, and with his quest for power he will go after her, she's Alto's weakness."

"How many are with him?"

I sigh. "I wish I knew. I can't be sure. I know for sure the two goons that tried to follow us and probably would have killed us, are part of it, but I can't say if there are others. Damaris doesn't have a mate. He does have blood children but most of them don't want anything to do with him."

"The question is this. Is Damaris acting alone and only targeting vampires or do other members of different factions have the same intentions?" Kane asks everyone. "The information we have from some of the shifters tells us he isn't working alone but we don't know how many others are involved."

I look at Alex. "So what you said about other factions joining together to form a new one could be what's going on?"

"Maybe. I can't speak on behalf of the witches, but we've started to notice some of the shifters have been acting weird. Are they under a spell or part of a cult that wants to rebuild our community? Anything is possible. For now, and until we have more intel, I don't know more than that."

Everybody starts talking at the same time. "Are you saying a witch is behind this?" one of the younger witches asks.

"No, but they could be part of it." Alex tries to explain what he'd meant which causes an argument to break out between him and the three witches.

"Stop, everyone!" Kane interrupts the debate. "We won't find a solution if we continue like this. Ross, Kass, what have we got?" Ross looks at Kane and Kane frowns back at him. "Don't start that bullshit with me and all that 'this is classified' shit. You know this could be bigger than the agency. So start talking."

"Fucking half-demon."

Kane shows his fangs, and by instinct, I show mine. He's my mate, and I need to protect him.

Ross sighs as he sees we aren't going to back down. "Fine. So far what we have is this. A new faction seems to be forming. It seems they don't just want to exist but they want to conquer all the other factions. From what we've discovered, even within the agency, we've had people whose behavior can only be described as unusual and then they disappear. Not just with whatever secrets they know but also with a weapon that can be used to capture any kind of species if needed."

I look at them, that's fucking bad. "I overheard Damaris talking about a new order with some people. I thought it was only within the vampire community. I didn't think it was anything like this. Everyone is in danger."

Kane puts his hand on my shoulder. "Panicking won't help. We need more intel from the other factions. We need to know if they are experiencing the same things we're talking about."

"Could the evil forces be with them?" one of the witches asks Kane.

"Maybe. We don't know. Information is coming in slowly, but it's a possibility. At this point, anything is possible," Kane replies.

I look at him and wonder what we've got ourselves into. I'm happy I've found my mate, but the rest has me worried.

11. KANE

THIS WHOLE SITUATION IS OFF AND WE TALK FOR A time, tossing ideas back and forth. The witches tell us they'll keep us informed with anything they find before they leave. My team has already left to continue their search and Lizbeth is looking through the window deep in thought. It's a lot of information to process in one night, and we're still not sure if any of it is correct.

"I'm happy you found your mate."

I turn and see Alex. "Thanks, man. That means a lot to me."

He smiles. "I don't know how or when, but hopefully one day it will be my turn."

I laugh and look at him. "I hope it's sooner rather than later, my friend."

"I know you will protect her whatever the cost. What's your plan?"

I sigh, do I have one? "I don't know. The only thing I'm sure of is that I must keep Lizbeth alive for all our sakes."

She turns and smiles at me. I can see the worry in her eyes

but also faith in me and us. "You're talking about me," she says as she walks over to stand by my side.

I grab her waist and pull her closer and kiss her cheek. "Maybe. Alex told me he's jealous I found my mate."

Alex laughs. "Maybe, but more envious than jealous if I'm totally honest."

"You will find your mate one day. I didn't think I'd find mine." She grabs my waist harder as I kiss her on top of her head.

"I know. You're not the only one to tell me that. Are you both staying at the hotel for the night?"

"If you don't mind, Alex, and part of the day. We'll leave tomorrow night. I'm waiting for my team to get back to me with a safe house for us until we catch him. My place has obviously been compromised."

"Hey, don't worry, man. You've got one here. The alpha asked me earlier, and I thought it would be the case now your place has been compromised."

I know my place is secure, but they know where I live and going back there isn't an option at the moment. "Thanks. The same room as usual?"

"No, my alpha gave you the top suite as it's suitable for a vampire. It's a special room." He takes us there and the corridor is dimly lit. "We've got security covered so don't worry. The alpha never liked that group apart from the one that was in trouble. None of them have ever been here and don't know how things work."

I shake his hand. "Thanks, no need to bring blood but can you bring us some food? I figure my mate will need to drink tonight and I need to be at the top of my game for her."

Alex smiles and leaves us in front of the door.

"Wow, this is gorgeous," she says as we enter the room.

"Alex and the alpha have given us the best. Don't worry, it

has a system to close the blinds so we'll be covered during the day."

She jumps on the king-sized bed. "How long we will stay here?"

"Not long. My team knows I need a safe house and we can't put this place in danger. I know the alpha will do his best to keep everyone at bay but other people are here, and I don't want to scare them more than they already are."

"I agree."

"So, we'll leave tomorrow night. I should have more information by then but for now, we'll wait for our food, and we'll get some sleep. If you need anything, you know what to do." I wiggle my eyebrows at her.

She smiles. "Maybe, but I think you need to remind me. My brain is fried and I'm on information overload."

"Don't worry. We'll get out of this in one piece. I'll make sure of it."

She's walking toward me when someone knocks at the door. I check through the peephole and see Alex. I open the door and he enters with not one, but two big trays of food for us.

"I know the big guy needs his food. You know what to do if you need anything?"

"Yes, don't worry. We'll be fine."

Alex nods and heads for the door. "Before I leave, if something happens you know the code right, Kane?"

I look at him. "Yes, it's fine."

He leaves us alone and I take a sandwich from the tray and eat.

Lizbeth wraps her arms around me from behind. "You need fuel?" she asks with a wicked smile.

"Yeah, I do. Especially if my mate wants her fill of me later."

"I will, but for now I want you to hold me. I've got too

much on my brain."

"Do you need distracting?" I turn in her arms and look into her eyes. I can see how tired she is. "The sun will be up soon. I'm closing the blinds. Go to bed, and I'll be there soon."

She agrees without arguing proving how tired she is. After securing everything and the main door, I grab my cell just in case I get any messages while we are asleep.

I take her in my arms and soon after she falls into a deep sleep. I'm trying to adjust to my new life as a night owl. A half-demon can go a few days without sleeping if they eat enough. I stroke her hair. Something is coming but what and why? The first thing that comes to mind is power but why are the different factions working together? The big unanswered question is—are they working together or are they working for someone else that's promised them each something different?

We can cohabit together, the neutral zone is the proof of that, but each faction needs their space too. Even between factions within the same species there can be tension or hatred, especially between vampire families. Werewolves and vampires have been in a war for a century or more which leaves me perplexed as to what has changed. Why are they working together now? What other species are working together?

My phone buzzes and I head to the lounge area so I don't disturb Lizbeth. I've received a text message from Kass telling me the safe house north of Montreal is ready for us. I know which one she means. The building itself is a fortress. I text back and put some food in the fridge for when we wake. Heading back to the bedroom, I place the phone on the nightstand again and climb into bed.

I close my eyes, but my head is still spinning wondering how long it will be until we have answers.

12. DAMARIS

"WHERE THE FUCK SHE IS?" I'M IMPATIENT. AT THIS point the bitch will ruin everything if we don't find her soon.

"We lost them. We think they went back to the hotel."

That fucking hotel again, I'll need to take care of the alpha myself if he keeps getting in my way. "Fine, send someone there!" Stan, one of my men, looks down. "What?" I ask.

"The shifters know us and expect us to be trouble. They won't open the doors for us. That hotel is full of booby traps, including an ultraviolet weapon."

I slapped him in the face. "Fuck! That fucking alpha is pissing me off. We need to put that hotel down."

"Sorry, boss, but even members of the SIA are there protecting them."

Oh. If the Supernatural Intelligence Agency is there, that isn't good. "Did you get in contact with our associate?" I need backup and information here.

"Yes, their reply was 'stay low and wait'."

I knew they would say something like that. The sun is almost up. "I need to sleep, but I will wake early. Be ready.

We'll plan for the rest. We need her gone, to be ashes. You both understand." They nod and leave me alone in my room.

"Uncle?"

I turn and see him, that bastard of kid that cut me from my right to have power over the family. "Yes, my dearest Bran?"

He smiles at me. For a vampire, he's young and naive in a lot of aspects. "Do you have a problem, uncle?"

"No. We're dealing with that traitor bitch vampire that was your plaything for a few years."

He smiles. "Can I have the pleasure of helping. I will be happy to play with Lizbeth again."

"Thirsty for blood, my nephew?"

"Maybe. She was a pain in my ass for so many years, and I want to be sure she's gone."

I grin. This could be interesting. "Great, we'll keep her for you. My team needs to snatch her first and bring her here. She will suffer the pain of a final status with us. I know a couple of your bitches want her head."

"They can play, but I want to give the final blow. I demand it."

That fucker. "Granted. I'll let you know when she's inside our walls."

He nods and leaves. The more people that are involved, the less I need to dirty my hands. I lock my door, it's dawn and I need to sleep. I stretch out on the bed with a smile on my face. The future holds a lot of good things for me.

13. LIZBETH

NIGHT HAS FALLEN ONCE MORE AND I WAKE with my mate beside me and smile. I didn't think any of this would happen to me, but now I want to grab it with both hands and not let go.

"Hey!" I touch his face wanting to know him more, that side of him I didn't think I'd have.

He opens his eyes at my touch. "Hey, you. It's night." He stretches himself and brings me closer to him.

"So, what's next?" I ask.

"That's easy. We go to headquarters. We need more information. After that, we'll hide until I know for sure it's safe for us."

I move on top of him and he strokes my back. "Just that?"

He looks at me puzzled. "Why? Do you want something else? You'll have your mate all to yourself until we know."

I sigh, and move off him.

"What?" he asks.

"I want to fight back. I don't want to have to hide. That will give him leverage over us."

He sighs and pinches his nose. "Maybe, but I rather you were safe. For me, for us."

I play with his hair. "I know, but that doesn't mean it's the best idea."

He stands and paces in front of me. "You want to be a target? Bait? Never knowing where or when he's going to strike? Get hurt and maybe die?"

If I were human, I'd probably cry but vampires don't have the ability. We don't have water inside us, only blood. "I don't know. I'm sure we can come up with a plan."

He sits beside me on the bed. "Whatever decision we make, it's like flipping a coin, and that coin is too precious for me to risk. We'll go to headquarters and try to come up with the best solution for all of us." I kiss him on the cheek in thanks. "But if anything makes me uncomfortable for any reason, we're going directly to the safe house. For now, we'll work with the groups that want to know the truth, but we're going to have to wait and see what our next move will be once we get more information."

I smile. "That's all I ask. I want to participate in taking Damaris and the others out of commission. As you said, we don't know how deep this thing goes and who is heading it. We can do it with the help of the others." I put my arms around his neck and rest my head on his chest. "Believe me, I want to live and have a life with you. I don't want to die but I want to help too. I'm not fragile and I can fight and I understand that against a vampire that is centuries old my chances of winning are nil, but you'll be there too, and I have faith in you to keep me safe."

He kisses me and is going deeper when his phone buzzes. "Fuck, I want to wake up every night like this. It's time to go. Alex just buzzed to say a car is waiting for us outside. He will take us back to HQ."

I move off the bed and head naked to the bedroom. I find

clothing that Alex probably left before we arrived in the room, I bend over to pick it up as Kane comes up behind me. "Hey! Don't slap my butt!"

He laughs. "Well, that butt belongs to me, and you were showing too much of it. If you want to get this over and done with and be back in a room with only the two of us, you had better move faster."

I laugh. That's one of the things I love about him—he's able to have fun and be serious at the same time. I increase my speed, not to my maximum but enough to satisfy him. "There, happy?"

He comes to me and puts his arm around my waist. "That vampire speed always amazes me." He grabs my hand, and we head down to the lobby to find the alpha there waiting for us.

"Kane, good luck! Don't forget you're always welcome here."

They shake hands, and I smile. "Thank you. It's appreciated."

He smiles and leaves us.

We head outside and Alex opens the door of the car before jumping in the driver's seat and starting the engine. "I hope they don't follow us this time. I don't want to scratch my jag's paint."

I don't reply. I hope we make it to the SIA Headquarters without someone trying to kill us.

"Don't jinx it, Alex. Let's go and keep our fingers crossed."

I look outside and behind me for the next few minutes, trying to spot if anyone is behind us.

"Relax we're almost there, and no one is following us. You haven't seen anything, and I can't hear anything either. I'm also guessing Alex can't smell anything different."

Alex smiles at us via the rear mirror. "Nothing."

"Maybe he's scared."

I laugh. "Well, if you think that you don't know him that's for sure."

Kane pulls me closer. "You're right, I don't, but after tonight I will. The agency is compiling a full report on the top members we know of and others that could be involved."

I look at him. "OK. I wonder what they're hiding."

He kisses me briefly. "Don't worry, love. You can tell us if we miss anything, you've been close to them for a century."

That's true. My heart is racing, but I cross my fingers that everything will be fine and Damaris will be exposed and maybe killed in the process. I take Kane's hand and look out the window. I can see the building that contains the SIA headquarters. The sign is big enough. We've arrived without being chased, and I wonder what we'll discover once we're inside.

14. KANE

WE ARRIVE AT HQ WITHOUT ANYTHING UNUSUAL happening and I can breathe again. The elevator door opens, and Ross and Kass are there waiting for us.

"You took your time." I laugh, I would have taken more time if I'd had my way with my mate. "Come, and you too, Alex. We've got some new info."

He locks the car and follow us. "My alpha isn't here," Alex says.

"We know, but we've advised him, and he said you were the best to handle everything," Kass replies as we enter the elevator.

We stay silent until the doors open again.

I leave the elevator first and head to the conference area in the middle of the control room. I can see that witches and other species already there.

"Come," Kass says.

I show Lizbeth to her chair and put myself behind her. Alex decides to sit beside her.

"So, now all of us are here, we're going to start," Ross says.

I look at the screen in front of us and see a photo of

Damaris as Kass begins to speak. "As per Lizbeth's information, we know Damaris is head of a new group. We don't know for sure what they want, but we know he wants power and to become the head of his family. That's enough to make him want to move against his blood."

Another picture appears. "This is Alto, he's been the head of the Sutton family for at least a millennia, but again, we aren't sure exactly how long. Two hundred years ago, he found his mate. She's human but because she drinks his blood it has extended her life in the process, and they were able to have a son who is a full vampire."

I look at Lizbeth as her ex, Bran appears on the screen.

She looks back and smiles. "You're the one I love," she says out loud.

I want her so badly and need to hide the fact my dick has reacted to her words. *Fuck.* I'm hard just from hearing her say those words. She laughs realizing my predicament. "I love you too, but you will pay for that," I reply.

"Phew. It's suddenly got hot in here!! Stop it, you two," Alex complains beside us.

We laugh, and Ross looks at us. "Are you finished?"

I grin. "No, but I will later."

She turns around and slaps my arm. I know deep inside she isn't offended over my teasing.

"We don't think that Alto and his son are involved. What we do know is that Damaris has a few followers, remember these two?" I growl seeing the photos on the screen. "Well, they're his henchmen, and we know they're involved in the new organization. Am I right?" Ross asks my mate.

"You're correct so far."

"Good, but we also know that each week those three were at the bar in the far east area of Montreal, almost like they were having a regular meeting. We've had them on our watch list for a few weeks now. What you told us, Lizbeth, only confirmed what we already suspected. What we don't know for certain, but strongly suspect, is that they have a few humans who want to be transformed in their group. That way they can be on watch and do missions when their master is asleep or unable to be there."

"That's weird. Usually, when a human becomes a vampire, Alto will give them a test to carry out. Well, that's what he did with me and others I know of," my mate replies.

"Maybe, but Damaris wants to change that rule. Since we think Alto doesn't know about this, he's made promises he may not be able to deliver on. The only problem is it's proving difficult to track them. It could be anybody at this point. Not only is The Black Lotus open to mixing species like the others, but there has been other activity there that could lead us to this group."

"I can add more to this," Gwen says.

Ross makes a sign for her to continue.

"We've had a few witches and wizards that disappeared for a few months and then came back, but they are changing. We can see that something had happened by their aura and magic signature. From what we know, some of the others that were missing never came back."

"But you can trace them by their magic signature?" I ask.

"That's the problem. Their signature is gone or has been replaced. We can't say which for now. We don't know all the details, but as I said yesterday, we know from the warrior witch covens that more objects are calling for help which is causing them more work than usual and they aren't having much time between calls."

"Can you tell us more?"

Gwen looks at me. "Yes, one of the reasons we're here is to put our knowledge together. You now know a warrior witch must answer a call from a magical object that doesn't want to be found when someone or something evil is close to finding it. Each magical object has a way to backtrack to a warrior witch that is trained specifically in those objects."

"Sorry, I'm not sure I'm following," my mate says.

"Well, specifically are they to retrieve the particular object. A witch could be a stone specialist and will only receive a call from stone objects. If a magic book called, it would be only heard by a warrior witch that specializes in magic books."

"What you're saying is that there could be more than one witch on the same case if there's more than one magic item to retrieve?" I ask.

"Yes, that could happen. The calling is to the object itself. At the moment it's different. The callings are happening one after another. That has never happened in the past. It's one of the reasons we started to suspect something wasn't right in the community. We also received a call from the Elders, when they felt a change in the magic energy."

"Who are they?" I ask.

"They are our sages if you like. They've been here since the beginning of magic."

Alex whistles. "That old. I guess even older than Alto?"

"True, but we don't know much about them. Only that they are part of the witches community, and they are like big libraries we can question."

"Let's get back to those witches. You said the situation isn't normal?"

"No it isn't, and since the Elders asked us to work with your agency, it's getting worse."

I go over everything again, trying to put the pieces together. We've had people that disappear for a time and come back but are changed, others never came back. The magic calls are from objects that could maybe help in a revolution and their callings to the warrior witches are increasing.

It's something to think about. "It all smells a bit fishy to me. Alex, anything happening in the shifter world?"

Alex rises from his chair. "From what we know, some shifters went missing and became so feral when they came back we had to put them down. We don't know why it happened. We don't know if there's a pattern with it all, but I do know my alpha is worried about his pack, others are too. We have some physical abilities, but we can't compete against magic. Capturing a shifter takes a lot of magic energy, but it's feasible."

I put my hand on my friend's shoulder. "Other than that?"

He looks at us. I know he knows more than he wants to tell us. "We captured a fae a month ago."

"A fae?" The witch asks.

"Yes, she was damaged. We tried to save her but we couldn't in the end. She relayed some information to us. She could open anything that was encased in metal and had a lock on it. She didn't want to participate, but was beaten when she refused."

I look at Lizbeth. I'm pretty sure Alex was the one that took her to the hotel.

"From what we know and from what she was able to tell us, someone or a group of paranormal individuals, want control of the community. She didn't know the reason why. The only thing she said is that they were looking for an artifact to help them. She also told us that in her faction she was a princess. When my alpha found out, we tried everything we could to save her."

15. LIZBETH

A PRINCESS. I look at Alex and Kane. *What does all this mean?* The fae are reclusive and rarely mingle with other species. How were they able to capture one? Did they use the magical object Ross mentioned yesterday that could be used to capture any paranormal being?

"That's weird. It's hard to capture a fae of any kind," Kane tells everyone.

"We know and for someone in her position to be hurt like that..." Alex answers.

"They possibly used a forbidden object to weaken her, to make her more willing to do their job. That would explain how they were able to capture her," one of the witches said.

"Do you think one of those objects is in their possession?" I ask the witch.

"Maybe. I will have to inform the coven about this." She turns to Alex then. "What did you do with the body?"

Alex looks at the witch. "We put her back close to her gate, the closest we could without them noticing."

I look around the room. "Maybe even within the fae weird things are happening. How can we contact them?"

"If they want to corrupt the fae then it's bad. I need to ask some of the warrior witches and verify some failed missions, and that kind of object can be traced. The fae community will be aware of their dead princess. Her family definitely knows. They have some sort of beacon with these things. We don't know much about them, but we do know this."

I want to ask more questions, but my brain has stopped working. What do they want? The question always comes back to that.

"We need to contact as many other factions as possible. Some will be difficult to reach. Especially the vampires after what happened with my mate and the fact they don't like us."

The witches laugh. "Maybe, but you know your agency can do the impossible."

Alex looks at me. "We'll need to send a team. Maybe Ross and Kass can go instead of you since you're involved with her. They'll know and will want to kill you for touching her."

I continue to think, but Alex is right. "I don't want to hide," I say out loud. "Hiding won't solve anything."

One of the witches comes over to me. I've never seen a witch like her before, but her magic energy surrounds me. "We know you want to help. I can read it but now is not the time. You will have your turn but let us try to figure out what's happening first."

I sigh feeling useless.

"We will meet again in a few days. We'll keep in touch. Kane, you need to check if the demon dimension is involved because if they are, that implies that maybe another evil dimension could be luring individuals for their gain."

"True, I will. I don't sense anything yet, but that doesn't mean they won't in the future."

The witch nods at him and the three of them leave.

"Well, instead of having more information, it's getting muddier," Alex says as he stands beside me.

"Maybe but we are in the mud like never before, I guess," I answer him.

He smiles at me and heads over to my mate. They talk but my head is spinning. I need to know what is happening within the vampire faction. Maybe another clan leader can help. Alex leaves followed by Ross and Kass.

I look at my mate. "What is next?"

He sighs and takes me in his arms. "We continue to dig. We'll place people to ask questions without revealing too much."

He puts his arm around my back and heads back down a corridor. "It's almost sunrise and you need to sleep. We'll stay here for now and see if we get more information."

I nod at him and let him show me the way. I don't say much, my head is too heavy to stay up as exhaustion hits me. I lie on the bed, and he follows me. I crawl over him and fall into a dreamless sleep.

SOMEONE KISSES me on my neck, and I smile. I know who it is. "Hey."

He kisses me. "Hey, sleepyhead, get ready. We have a visitor. She's a vampire."

I look at him surprised. "How so?"

He looks at me. "She came to us. She heard about your story, and she may be able to help us catch Damaris. She's part of internal affairs within the vampire faction."

"Wow, really? I've never met anyone from there before. I've heard rumors about a different kind of vampire but I didn't believe them."

He smiles at me. "Come, let's go meet her. Don't worry though, security will be around just in case."

I pull my clothes on. "According to the rumors, they're easy to identify. They've got a special tattoo on their face which is part of their organization and tells everyone who they are."

He grabs my hand, and we head back to the meeting room. He enters and I follow behind him. I see her—she has the tattoo on the side of her temple—the sun symbol—and I gasp, realizing the rumors are fact.

"Hello, Lizbeth. I'm glad to finally meet you."

"And you are?"

She smiles and brushes back her long auburn hair. "Sorry, I'm Casey. I'm part of internal affairs. Something nasty is going on within the vampire clan and I'm in charge of investigating it. Damaris is at the top of the list as the one behind it. We have a lot of information on him. I'm happy to see he didn't capture you and that you're mated now. That will make things more difficult for him."

"Sorry to ask this question but you're a vampire, right?" Kane dares to ask.

She smiles and looks at me. "She knows what I am. She's never met one of us, but she knows the myth." She looks at me amused.

"Yes, she is, but she's special. Inside our community, they are a legend, but I didn't think they were real. As I said, I didn't believe the rumors. She's what we call a daywalker. It's why they're part of the organization. They don't have any blood family whatsoever."

She sits down with her pen and paper waiting for me to do the same.

"A daywalker? What does that mean?"

"It means exactly what it sounds like, I'm a vampire that can go outside during daylight. Shall we start?"

***** TO BE CONTINUED*******

You want to know read Casey's story, you will find it in the
book call Blood Rebellion. Here a glimpse.

SUPERNATURAL INTELLIGENCE AGENCY WORLD BOOK ONE
BLOOD REBELLION
USA TODAY BESTSELLING AUTHOR
NADINE TRAVERS

BLOOD REBELLION

It sucks being a daywalker but I've got a vampire to catch.

A rogue vampire is on the loose, and it's Casey's mission to drag him back to Vampire Internal Affairs headquarters to face justice. It's a job only a daywalker like her can handle, and she's the best there is.

While tracking down Damaris, Casey uncovers a new threat within the supernatural community that makes no sense, and she teams up with the SIA (Supernatural Intelligence Agency) to help her solve the mystery and bring Damaris to justice.

But things keep getting deeper and muddier, and as she unveils a decade-old conspiracy, she discovers more secrets than she was expecting and one that will change her life forever.

Damaris calls it a rebellion. It seems that some in the paranormal community are fed-up with the factions dividing the different species, and they are ready to destroy everything in order to shift the balance of power.

With the combined powers of her supernatural crew, she only has one chance to discover the true villain—but is she willing to risk it all in a dangerous game?

This is a paranormal detective series/supernatural thriller for readers who like thriller-based urban fantasy with snarky heroines who won't give up on her mission.

1. CASEY

I LOOK AT MY COMPUTER MONITOR AND FROWN. A week has passed since my meeting with Lizbeth and Kane—my contacts at the Supernatural Intelligence Agency, or SIA for short—and there's still no sign of Damaris. "You think it's a real lead?"

I look up at the question and my eyes meet Sophia's, I immediately know from the look on her face she's trying to stir up trouble. "Why wouldn't it be?"

She leans against my desk. "Well, because since you met with them, nothing has happened and everything in the neighborhood is quiet."

I roll my eyes. "It's the best lead we have right now. I still have things to check, and the SIA Team can provide me with information we don't usually have access to."

She twitches her mouth. "If you say so."

I look back at my monitor and continue to read the email, ignoring her in the hopes she'll go away. I guess she finally gets the message I don't want to talk about when she sighs and goes back to her own desk. Yes, this is my life. Not only am I part of the vampire faction's Internal Affairs but I'm also a daywalker, which sucks sometimes.

The Vampire faction's Internal Affairs is like a human police force. Centuries ago, the paranormal community decided to create a separation between the various groups on Montreal Island. Members of other species can't stay inside a different species territory but are allowed to pass through on their way somewhere else. Daywalkers are different. We don't have a blood allegiance toward a specific faction as we are born after our mothers are bitten. The bite results in early labor and we tend to be born in a rush before our mother dies from the blood loss. We are born with the abilities of a vampire thanks to that bite, which includes the need to drink blood, but we can go outside during daylight. Hence why we are called 'daywalkers'. Not very creative I know, but it works for who we are.

My phone rings and a quick check of the caller ID shows me Kane is finally calling, so I pick it up. "Hello, Kane, do you have any news?"

He sighs. "None. I think Damaris is either dead or hiding until he can get away."

"Is Alto searching for him?"

There's a small silence on the other end of the phone. "From what we've heard, yes, he is."

That's what I fear. Alto Sutton, head of his family and Damaris's blood brother, now views him as a traitor. Death is the only way for them to resolve their issues now.

"Well, I know he's not dead. Alto would know in his blood if he was. He's hiding, and we need to find him before Alto does."

"Shit, Casey, could it be he's not even in vampire faction land?" His voice shows his apparent frustration at the thought.

"Maybe. We have to consider he's in the neutral zone or

hiding God knows where. With the different faction members becoming involved with the new movement, we're starting to get more information."

The reason for that is government representatives from each faction are working together for a change. The information we've been getting is telling us something—or someone —wants to cause the factions and communities to collapse, for the divisions between us to cease, and that includes the human community who don't even know we exist.

"You'll keep me posted?"

"Yes, of course, I will, Kane. Let me know if you hear anything on your end as well."

"Thanks. Liz says hi as well. Talk to you soon."

I hang up and grab my coat.

"Where are you going?" My boss Grant comes into my office. He isn't a daywalker like us, and there's something about him I don't like.

I turn around and force a bright smile. "Investigating. We need to find Damaris and whoever is behind the new movement."

"You need to let go of the Damaris case. We have other open cases that need your attention."

Right now, I want to punch him. "Grant, you don't have a say on this. You know I'm on a special assignment. The SIA asked us to investigate and specifically requested me. You'll need to give any other cases to someone else."

"Lucky for you they require your services but don't forget who you work for. The investigation won't last forever, and after that nobody will ask for you." He turns around then and heads to his office.

I sigh. Daywalkers don't have a choice where we work. Internal Affairs is our only option as no one else can investigate during the day. Luckily for me, I'm the best, and Grant knows he can't remove me from a case or the team. Sophia looks at me and smirks. I can't stand her either. I suspect those two are sleeping with each other, but without proof, I can't report them. Maybe if they push me too hard I might be able to come up with something I can do.

My phone buzzes then, grabbing my attention away from thoughts of Grant and Sophia.

I know where he is. The message is from an unknown person.

Who? I send back and wait for a reply.

Damaris. Fuck, who is this?

Who are you and where is he? I hit send again and study my phone.

You will know when the time comes. Continue as you are, you're on the right path.

I try to send another message wanting to know more, but the phone says the number doesn't exist. It's a fucking burner that the sender has just disabled.

I punch in some numbers. "Harry!"

He sighs before speaking. "What do you want, Casey?"

"I need something from you. Can you trace a phone from a text message sent to me?"

"I'm on a rush job, you know the boss."

The desire to punch Grant rises again, but I pinch my nose instead. "Am I right in assuming he's told you not to help me?"

I'm greeted with silence for a few seconds. "Casey, not all of us have what you have. He's put me on a project, said it's my top priority."

I feel for Harry. He's our best hacker and is excellent at tracking people on the town's CCTV cameras.

"Did he say you shouldn't help me?"

"He said you have other resources to use, and other agents are my priority."

Lucky for that bastard he isn't in front of me right now. "Fine."

"Casey, you know I'd help if I could."

"Sure, Harry, I know. It's fine." I hang up. I need to contact Kane's group as they're my only option right now. I pick up the phone and call Kane back.

"Hey, Casey. Miss me already?"

"Kane, I have a problem." His laughter stops at my words. "Internal Affairs cut my resources. They said I have to use you guys since I'm working your case."

"You're kidding? Your boss really didn't do that, did he?"

"Yes, he did. I don't know what his agenda is, but he's not happy I'm working the case with you."

"What do you need?"

"I received a weird text, and I need you to hack it and trace who sent it."

"What did the message say?"

"It said they know where Damaris is, but that I need to wait."

"Fuck, really? Don't worry. I'll get Greg to call you." With that, Kane hangs up.

I look up and wish we had windows so I could see the view of downtown Montreal. The city is divided among the factions, but downtown is the neutral zone, and each group has its own hotel, restaurant, and night club. The city is gorgeous during daylight, and luckily vampires can't witness that. All I can catch during daylight are goons. They are servants to vampires who promise to turn them in exchange for their loyalty.

The phone rings again, interrupting my thoughts.

"Hey, Casey, it's Greg. Kane said you needed something?"

I smile. I've spoken to him before, but we've never met face to face. He's a computer nerd and one of the best I know. "Yes. Can you access my text messages to trace a phone?"

"That's something a kindergartener can do. Too easy, but Kane said it's important, so I'll do it."

"Stop whining and do what you have to. If my guess is right, you'll have a more complicated job soon." I hang up. Physically he's a man, but emotionally he comes across as more like a teenager who's never grown up.

I look around the near-empty office. It's close to noon, and I need to eat. As a daywalker, I do both—eat food and drink blood. I leave the office and head to my favorite Chinese restaurant in Chinatown, which is at the far limit of the neutral zone. It's time to go hunting.

A couple of weeks later, I'm back at the Chinese restaurant. I never made it back to Internal Affairs after leaving for lunch. Greg was able to track the phone the messages came from but it was a burner and had been destroyed. We were able to get a general location though, and I've been chasing lead after lead ever since.

A waitress greets me as soon as I enter the restaurant. "Miss Casey, your regular table?"

Most of the shops and restaurants in Chinatown are owned by vampires, and I always go during the day when there are no other vampires inside. I doubt if I went at night, I would get my regular table.

I sit on the chair, and she leaves me alone. She knows my order and that it never changes. This place has the best noodles in the city—a fact is borne out by the fact it's becoming more crowded by the minute. I can learn a lot, sitting there, listening to different conversations. My table is near the kitchen but central enough within the restaurant where I can hear couples, families, and singles talk as they eat. Even though they are human and could be talking about fake news, it can still be valuable information.

"Here, Miss Casey, enjoy." The waitress delivers my big bowl of noodle soup. It's too hot to eat just yet, so I close my eyes to listen. Daywalkers have all the advantages of a full vampire, including heightened hearing. I think people in the restaurant believe I'm praying before my meal.

"Did you watch that video on YouTube last night?" a male voice says.

"No, I was asleep when you sent it. What was it?" Another higher-pitched male voice asks.

"It's of a vampire in that club, The Black Lotus. You know the one."

Now I open my eyes and pinpoint the voices sitting a few tables to my left. They are talking or rather whispering, to each other, and I see the redhead is the one who sent the video, his friend is blond.

"You need to watch it."

Both of them take out their phones and start searching, probably on YouTube. "Man, the video has been removed. I'm telling you, it was a vampire drinking blood live on camera," the redhead says.

"It was probably part of a movie. Why else do you think YouTube removed it? Copyright, man."

If only they knew, I think and smile. *Mental note to self, you need to go to The Black Lotus tonight.* It belongs to the Thompson family, more specifically Jeremy Thomson, who is one of Alto's friends from another vampire family. Alto, in turn, owns The Wicked Club.

I finish my meal, pay my invoice, and head outside. As I start to walk I see him—it's a face I know by heart and one I've seen several times before. He's one of Damaris's goons, one of those humans who serve a vampire in the hopes they'll be transformed if their master is happy with their work. I decide to follow him and look around for a taxi, hoping this guy will at least lead me to Damaris's secret warehouse. I see one and head over to ask the driver if he's free.

He motions for me to jump in. "Where're you going, miss?"

"I'm wondering if you want to make a lot of money today, my friend."

His eyes widen. "If it's legal."

"It is."I point to the car. "Do you see that SUV in the street to your left?"

"Yes."

"Follow him, and I'll give you this." I show him my cash, which is all pink notes.

"At your service, ma'am." He watches the SUV pull out and starts to follow him.

"Don't lose him."

"I know downtown Montreal by heart. Don't worry, I won't lose him."

With that, he follows the SUV until it stops at a warehouse in the Old Port.

2. DAMARIS

THE NIGHT HASN'T ARRIVED, BUT I KNOW IT'S coming as I wake and look around my temporary room. *That fucking Lizbeth*. She and her mate too, both will pay for what they've done. She will die, and even if Bran wants to be the one to kill her, I've lost too much, and she's my prize. Luckily for me, my nephew still keeps me informed on what is happening inside the family home.

I hear someone knock and tell them to come in. My gorgeous little lover enters. She's not my mate but fucking a faerie and tasting their blood is amazing.

"I see my lover is awake. Do you need to drink?"

Humans are stupid. A lot of paranormal creatures live in their world, but most of them aren't aware of that. "I'd prefer to have a taste of my lover tonight. That would be a good start."

She laughs, her crystal voice a mermaid song. I see other paranormal creatures as well as her to satisfy my thirst, but none of them know about each other, which serves my purpose. This place is temporary, and I need to contact the secret society about what has happened. Knowing them, they'll already know what's going on as they have eyes and ears everywhere. For now, though, my focus is on my faerie.

She's small against my frame as She joins me in bed, and I kiss her savagely, needing to bruise her lips. Faeries are tiny but should never be underestimated as they can be lethal. I need to fuck her, to bring a major orgasm to us both. I make her stand and remove her tiny dress and look at her, bare before me. I start to suck her tits, needing her to be ready because I need her tonight, her last night on this earth, not that she knows that. I put a finger in her pussy and start to play with it, my cock is already hard.

She smiles up at me. "Let me take care of you."

I don't want that, I just want something fast and to drink from her. I prevent her from touching me and swiftly enter her with my dick. She's turned on, I can smell her. I push her hair to one side and start to lick where her neck and shoulder meet. It's the fastest way to drink but also the quickest way to kill.

I tap her vein and start to drink. Faerie blood is like a drug for us. It gets us high as nothing else does.

"Damaris!" she screams, and I know my faerie has just come from the way she milks my dick, but I need more. Not only that, but she needs to be gone as she knows too much. I continue to drink. I'll be hearing from my contact soon, and I need to end her so she can't say anything to anyone.

"Damaris!"

Where before her scream came from pleasure, it isn't the case now. I'm able to taste her fear, and she starts to struggle in my arms, but she's becoming weaker and weaker with the loss of blood. I release her neck, and as I take the last drop of her blood, I look at her. before she was full of life, now she's still in death. I let her fall onto the bed, and I lick the blood from my lips with my tongue. I wish it could be different, but no one can ever know I was here.

My phone buzzes. "Damaris," I answer.

"Have you drunk? You need to come now," a male voice orders.

"Where?"

"We'll text you the coordinates. Just make yourself part of the crowd after we bring you into the secure area."

My phone buzzes, indicating a text arrived. "Fine, but I'll need a cleanup team here."

The man groans. "What have you done, you bloodsucker?"

"Watch it, dog. I killed her so no one can find me. I'll send the coordinates and the door will be unlocked."

"You watch it, bloodsucker. If it weren't for *her*, I'd leave you to fend for yourself. Okay, we'll do it. You have thirty minutes to get here. Otherwise, I've given my team orders to leave you."

He hangs up before I can answer. "That fucking dog, he better watch it."

I dress in jeans, a black t-shirt, and put my leathers on. I glance at the coordinates and reply with the ones for my location. I leave, unnoticed, and head back to downtown Montreal. During the tourist season, the Old Port is always full, and it's easy to move around unseen, helped by the partial moonlight. I keep my phone open until I find them.

"Damaris?"

I turn and see a big guy, who I know is a werewolf. "Yes."

He grabs my arm, and two others join him. "Follow us."

It's a step down for a vampire to put his safety in the hands of these dogs, but in these times we need extreme measures if we want to succeed.

We start to walk toward Maisonneuve Boulevard, where I see a limo waiting.

"Enter."

I do, and they follow me inside. "Where're we going?" I ask as the limo heads toward the highway.

"It's better if you aren't in the neutral zone. We have a safe house at the border between our territory and the neutral zone." By now, we are at Peel Street and Notre-Dame Street. West, at the limit of the neutral zone, and the limo stops at a small house. We get out, and the three werewolves tell me to follow them.

I enter, the smell of dogs disturbing me. I don't know what they use the house for, but I can tell they use it a lot. One of them heads toward the kitchen, and I follow him, the rest stay close to the door.

"So, Damaris, we finally meet face to face. I only wish it was under better circumstances."

I turn around recognizing the voice. "Donovan. I didn't think you'd be here to welcome me."

He sits on a chair and invites me to do the same. "The cleanup crew is taking care of your mess."

My jaws tighten. Normally I would never let him talk to me like this. "You're lucky you're one of her favorites. If it were up to me, I'd let you rot in your mess."

"I couldn't let her live and allow someone to interrogate her to get to us. Now is not the time." *Why do I need to justify myself to a dog?*

"Whatever. You've now given us a bigger issue. You can't try to kill one of yours and not have consequences. She escaped and has not only joined the SIA Investigation Team, but she's now mated with a half-demon that works there. That's fucking big. I thought you were the best in your family."

"You don't know anything about it. She got lucky. Not only did one of your dogs help Lizbeth, but the alpha is also helping her, which gives her a place to stay where no one can get to her."

"Watch it, bloodsucker. we need to get rid of her. Our Internal Affairs have started an investigation, and I think yours has as well."

I'm not surprised, those people at Internal Affairs are a pain. "Do you know who's behind it?"

"That's the problem. The head of your Internal Affairs has been bribed, but since the agent, they put on the case is helping Lizbeth, the Investigation Team is helping her."

"Who is it?"

Donovan sighs. "Casey."

"Fuck!" I want to hit something.

"Yes, my thoughts exactly. She's one of the best daywalkers and one of the most tenacious. She won't rest until you, and maybe us by association, are dead."

"We'll be able to restrain her." I turn at the female's voice. "Damaris, Donovan."

We both stand. "Sophia pleased to meet you in the flesh," I say. For a witch, she's gorgeous.

"Don't touch her," Donovan growls at me. His eyes are yellow, and his wolf is very close to being out.

"Stop, love, he doesn't know." Sophia touches Donovan, which tames his beast.

"Mates?" I ask.

She smiles at me. Our mates can be anywhere or anyone, either within our species or from another one, such as with Alto and his human.

"Yes, he is my mate." She leans in and kisses him before settling in his lap after he sits.

I sit on my chair. "What news do you have?"

"Well, having Lizbeth doing what she's doing isn't helping. We need to move faster than planned. Not only is the Investigation Team on our backs, but the witches' Internal Affairs are also involved now. I guess most of the factions have someone in their Internal Affairs working on it. The warrior witches are working like crazy, which means the Elders know something big is going on. We don't need that kind of publicity."

"I had no choice. Only now that dog Alex is helping her. I thought Lizbeth was alone and would be easy to grab after she saw me killing that faerie agent. I was wrong."

I see Donovan stroking Sophia's arms as he answers. "Maybe, but the one behind this has said we now only have a month. Before what happened with Lizbeth, only the warrior witches suspected anything, now the rest of the community is involved. Not only that, Kane is watching the demons to see if there is any activity there. We thought we had a wild card with you, but that's not the case anymore."

"What's our next step?"

Sophia kisses Donovan, and I can see their lust for each other. Vampires love to see desire and sex, even if there's no blood involved. "First, most of the Internal Affairs and the SIA know something is going on. One thing they don't know is where we're going to hit. We need that artifact to help us. It's the only way we can overthrow the community and have it the way we want. We need to recruit more people to our cause, and it doesn't matter from where. Those fucking warrior witches are a pain right now," Sophia tells me.

"Fine, which means we need to kill them."

She smiles at me then. "Well, the good thing is that when they get a call, we know where they're going and it'll be easy to set a trap for them. We've killed a few, but we need to kill more."

"One thing at a time. The others can take care of that. Now, what we can do?"

"We need Lizbeth and Kane dead. We need to regroup and focus on the neutral zone," Donovan tells me.

"What do you want from me?" I have a feeling I'll be bait, not only to lure Casey but also Lizbeth and Kane. Donovan starts to tell us his plan. It will be fun, just not for them, that's for sure.

3. CASEY

AFTER I PAY THE TAXI DRIVER, HE GIVES ME HIS card in case I need him in the future which is a first. Usually, humans don't want anything to do with me as they seem to sense there's something different about me and I give him an extra tip for his kindness. We've ended up in Montreal's Old Port, which is part of the SIA's territory, at one of the warehouses. I keep my distance from Damaris's men. Now I know their smell, they'll be easy to follow. The sun is intense even this late in the afternoon. I know I only have a short amount of time to do this, as Damaris will want them to report and bring him whatever it is they have for him.

It's harder to hide during daylight, and I look around for somewhere that allows me to be close, but still gives me some cover. I don't have my katana with me either, so I need to stay out of sight.

I watch the goon talking to a fat man as they unload boxes from the trunk of a car, a couple of Damaris's men watching as they work.

"So, my friend, do you think it'll be tonight?" the man says to Damaris's goon.

"Shut up! We don't talk about my master. I hope so, but that depends on him."

"Sorry, I don't know all the rules. The only thing that's good about this job is all the cash I make." Both continue to unload cases, and I'm guessing they contain something to trade.

"That's all you have?" Damaris's goon asks.

At his nod, he gives the fat one a small box, and when he opens it, his face lights up. I'm guessing there's something special inside. "Happy to do business with him. If he needs anything else, just let me know."

The goon closes the car trunk and shakes his hand before they walk to the front of the car. "I'll let him know."

"Did the master give you instructions where we will meet him tonight?" the fat one asks.

"Yes, but you can't come, he only wants me. He said he'll contact you tonight with another mission. I think you'll go far. You did a good job, but you need to keep your mouth shut. If not, he'll kill you so fast you won't even see it coming."

The fat one crosses his arms over his chest. "That's not fair, I've done a lot of his dirty work for him."

The goon sighs. "I know and believe me, he knows too. I told you how it works. You get introduced and give your allegiance to him. He'll give you a temporary mark until you're worthy of wearing the permanent one, and that's when you meet him again. Then you'll know you're a part of his inner circle like I am." With this, he shows the man his wrist. I can't see it, but I know Damaris. It'll be some sort of tattoo that doesn't stand out to other humans.

"Fine, I'll do what you say. I really want to be a vampire and immortal and fuck as much as I want."

The others laugh. "Well, my advice is to lose some weight

and train. When he changes you, you'll be stuck with that body forever, unless that's what you want."

The fat one glares at him. "I know. I'm starting at the gym tonight. I've hired a personal trainer."

The other guy slaps the fat one on the back. "Good decision, that's what I did when I started and look at me."

He does have a great body for a human, but I've seen better. Even though I don't have a partner, it doesn't mean I don't have sex.

"Fine."

"Keep your mobile close for when he calls. He doesn't like having to leave a message if you know what I mean."

The fat one nods and starts to walk away, passing close to where I'm hiding.

The first goon pulls out his phone again. "It's me." He kicks a little stone on the ground. "No, I got the money and the item... Well, the man didn't have any choice with my friend." He starts pacing, and I stay hidden, hoping to hear something useful. "Yes, he is eager, he said he's going to the gym." He laughs. "Yeah, I don't think he wants to stay that shape if you change him, Master."

A chill runs down my spine. Why would anyone want to please that fucking Damaris so badly?

"Yes, he'll wait for your call when you're ready." He hangs up, and I suspect he already knows where to go to meet Damaris. The goon hops into the SUV and heads off. It will be difficult to chase him as I'm on foot and I can't run at full speed. Since it's the afternoon, people will see me which can't happen.

But now I know his smell and his heartbeat. Vampires and daywalkers have a good sense of smell, although not as good as a shifter's. The one thing we know is that every pulse has a signature. We can match the heartbeat with the smell of their blood—every person's heartbeat is as unique as their finger-print. Our hearing is also one of the best, we match other species there. The goon will need to see Damaris somewhere in the neutral zone. If not, they could all be in trouble. I need to wait for night to fall. Today is the first half-moon, in the werewolf community, it brings almost as much excitement as a full moon as they start to feel the effects of the next full moon.

I continue to walk, following the smell when my phone rings and I see it's my boss.

"Do you have anything yet?"

"Since when do you want to know about my investigations? Especially after stopping anyone from helping me." I'm still pissed at him, and if he were in front of me right now, I'd hit him.

"Casey, I'm your boss. You need to report in. No one has heard from you in a couple of weeks."

I'm starting to have difficulty following the smell. Grant is affecting my concentration, that fucking bastard. "I'm work-ing, Grant, I'll call you later." I hang up, needing to concen-trate on the smell. My walk brings me close to Chinatown just as my phone buzzes again. "What?"

"Oops! Have I interrupted something?"

Fuck. "No, Kane, I thought you were my boss."

He chuckles. "I guess he's being a pain in the ass again. I was just calling to check in with you."

I smile. I know I need to get back to HQ, but it'll be on my terms. Grant can go fuck himself if he's not happy. "You have no idea."

I stop at the corner and see the man I'm chasing enter a small restaurant, but it's on the human side and out of the neutral zone. "Fuck!"

"You have a problem?"

"Yes. I followed one of Damaris's goons who led me to

Chinatown on the human side. From what I could hear, he's meeting Damaris tonight to give him something."

"Where?" Kane asks.

"I don't know. It'll be somewhere in the neutral zone, and if he uses a club, he'll avoid any Alto owns. He's looking for him too." I hate not having access to my resources at Internal Affairs, damn my boss. Why he doesn't want me to use them? Does he have something to hide?

"Are you there?" Kane asks.

"Sorry, just thinking. I'm wondering why my boss is being a pain in the ass. He's never involved himself in my missions before." I'm starting to think this whole thing is bigger than I anticipated. I know my boss is not a daywalker but a full vampire, although he's had no blood attachment to any vampires since his former maker was killed a century ago.

"Do you think he knows something?"

I sigh. "Maybe. I guess it's muddier than I anticipated. He's a vampire without his maker, which makes him similar to a daywalker in that he has no blood ties to any of the factions. I think that's why he's been interfering. As I said, he's never involved himself like he is now. Without my information, which is at our HQ, I can't dig." I continue to watch the building.

"Are you still in Chinatown?"

"Yes, but that doesn't mean he can't leave through the back. That zone is off-limits for us."

A portion of the town outside the neutral zone belongs to the humans. The government voted on that law. Some humans know about our community and us and are welcome to come into the neutral zone if they want to mingle with us, but we can't go to their part of the city. I think it's because we don't want to wake the human side of ourselves.

"I know, but come here. We can provide some equipment

for you to dig. I know it's not your stuff, but it's better than nothing. Greg would love to help you."

I smile. "Fine, I'm coming. You're there now?"

"Yep, my mate is asleep, but it'll soon be dark, and she'll be awake."

"Still can't change your way of life, Kane?"

"I have, but I was needed here. Lizbeth will join me later. How soon can you be here, Casey?"

I don't have a lot of options. Maybe one of the other daywalkers can help me figure it out. "I'll be there in thirty minutes. I'm on foot. See you later."

"That's fine, I'll let the administration know we're expecting you. Don't worry, we'll catch him, and thanks for helping us."

"It's nothing, Kane. I need someone to watch my boss too."

"Come here, and we'll discuss it. This is bigger than just one case. We're starting to discover that."

Maybe he's right. If my gut feeling is correct, it'll be hard to investigate when we don't know who we can trust. I head toward the Old Port and study the people as I walk. I'm amazed by the fact humans always seem to be chasing the clock. Like if they could walk quicker, it would be better for them. Maybe because their life is limited, it makes them grab life faster than us. Being immortal gives me plenty of time. The night rush hour is almost as crazy as the morning one.

I head to the building where the SIA is located. I enter the main hall and head to the elevator and hit the tenth floor. When the door opens the reception is right in front of me.

"Can I help you, Miss?"

I smile. "Yes, I'm Casey. I'm here to see Kane."

She looks at a piece of paper. "Yes, Casey, I'll call him, but you need to sign the visitor's list."

I comply, and a couple of minutes later, Kane enters the hall. "Come, the team will be here soon."

It's not ideal, but it's something. I need to contact my fellow daywalkers to see how the situation is going at HQ and see if I can lure someone to spy for me.

One step at a time, but I have a bad feeling about this whole thing.

4. THE LADY

"DO YOU HAVE NEWS?" I ask the group to gather around me.

"Boss, we do, but it's not good," the biggest male replies.

"Tell me, Steve."

"Casey is still looking for Damaris to bring him back to face justice for what he did. Knowing Casey, she won't stop until this is solved, which could lead her to us. Going after our henchmen is one thing, but we can't have her coming after us before everything is in place. We've just had word from our source that she's met with Kane and the others at the SIA headquarters. They don't know what's going on but thinks it's something big to do with Damaris."

I look at them. "Tell me why we haven't taken care of Damaris already? Why he is still walking around?" I know deep in my heart my plan is best for all of us, and for those that think I'm crazy.

"We need him for his connections in the vampire community. He's under Donovan's watch at the moment. He and his mate have orders that if Damaris is taken, to go for the kill."

I rub my temple. I've planned everything, but relying on others to put the plan in place causes headaches. "Fine, you know how to deal with it, Steve. If not, I will have your head." I start to pace, which helps me to think. All of them are looking at me, waiting. "We need to take things a step further. In other businesses, how are we going gathering the magical objects to help us in our quest?"

A woman approaches. "It's going well. We've got teams all around the globe tracking the objects we need."

I look at the maps. "And the warrior witches, Selena?"

She sighs. "They are there. Some of them are stopping us, but they can't be everywhere at once. Some of the warrior witches have joined us though and are helping us to find the objects."

I smile, pleased. "We need to rush the plan a little. Can our witches stop the calling?"

"We don't know for sure. We know we can put those objects elsewhere if something like that happens. We don't want them to find our location. They have enough on their plates at the moment, and I don't think they will come for those we were able to bring back."

I look at Selena, the fire witch. "You're sure?"

She smiles at me. "Yes, I am. From what I've heard, not many of the warrior witches are in a coven right now. It's only a select few that have the talent. That could work for us and against them."

"Maybe, but I want to be sure. How many are currently students at Paranormal University?" I need to know how many warrior witches we'll have to deal with within a couple of years.

"We don't know for sure. My contact said the Director is keeping key information private and being more secretive than usual. Helping Gorad in that area gave us more freedom since the SIA has to split their resources."

I'm able to go to different planes, which is how I met the dark wizard. He's stuck in his bindings, but when I told him about my idea, he agreed to help us. I smile, remembering our meeting.

"Tell me, Gorad, how are you going to help me, considering you're stuck in this dimension?"

He smiles, his dark eyes on me. "Easy, we need to divide the SIA to succeed. I need to kill people who have magic, especially witches. I have my people with me, but I need to release my bindings to send them to Earth to kill more and give me more magical energy."

"That's good. I'm preparing for a revolution. I want to reverse the paranormal community as we know it now. I want to bring a new order to this world. I need humans to understand we're at the top of the food chain, and they are slaves to us."

He chuckles. "I want the same thing, except I want it for myself."

I always knew the wizard existed, but I'd never thought I'd be able to find him. I smirk at him. "Not anymore. We are a group. You may be a powerful wizard, but you know the people that put you here can do it again."

"I know. So what's your plan?"

"It's simple. You keep the Paranormal University on edge, and the Supernatural Intelligence Agency will have to send one of their teams to the university. You keep them busy there. Oh, and can you kill a warrior witch student for me? That will help me a lot."

"Maybe but they're hard to kill. I need element witches and any half-breeds that have energy, even if they don't know it, to help me free myself."

"Fine, it will be a plus if you can kill a warrior witch for me."

"What will you do to help me?"

"Simple. I think you need a sacrifice, right?"

He nods at me.

"I'll corrupt a human to kill one witch, but you'll need to be the

one to contact him. Nobody needs to know my involvement in all this. For your first sacrifice, what type will help you to release one of your goons?"

"An elemental witch, she could be half-breed. That would also work."

I nod. "That will be done. I'll tell him the secret incantation so he will be able to prevent her from casting a spell to stop him and what he'll see is you. I'll take your form for that."

He smiles. "That's fine, but he needs to open the portal with that sacrifice, and I will need him for my pet on the other side. That's the only way I can send one of my henchmen to Earth, one for one."

"What's our next step?" Selena asks me.

"Gorad is helping us. He wants revenge, and I promised him a portion of the land for himself."

My second looks at me. "Are you sure the wizard is going to help us?"

I smile. "I put a spell on him. He may be powerful, but I'm more so, being cross-species help. He's taking care of the witches at the university. That's why I need to know if numbers start to go down. Especially in the warrior witch group."

She nods and leaves me.

It took me years to prepare for this, and now it's time. All the pieces are in place, and I'm ready to checkmate!

"My Lady?" Someone new enters the room.

"Come in, Donovan. What news do you bring me?"

He comes to stand next to me. "It's good news. You were right. We're working as a group, and it's showing. The way our community works now is obsolete. Not all of them will jump on the opportunity, though." He takes a breath. "Oh, and Damario is asking for you."

I'd almost forgotten about him. "I guess his plan didn't work then?"

Donovan sighs. "No. Now Lizbeth is mated to the half-demon that works with the Investigation Team they are also on the case. Between them and Casey, Damaris's plan had no chance."

I look at him. His mate is lucky, if he were single I'd have him in my bed. "Casey is a bitch and stubborn but we knew something like this would happen. Damaris is a weak link in our group. Vampires are not easy to convince, as they're tight with their history and they think they're above everyone. They think vampires are pure, which we know from history they aren't."I frown as a thought occurs to me. "Were you able to corrupt her boss?"

He grins at me. "We did, but she'd already made contact with Kane and he has put all his resources at her disposal."

I pace. "She's the best they have, you know. When she gets a job, she never gives up. That could be a problem."

"What are we going to do?" Donovan asks me.

"Simple, we keep a team on her, monitor her, and we screw with her investigation if possible, but if worst comes to worst—"

"Yes?"

"She'll capture Damaris, and we better hope she never finds out what's happening inside her Internal Affairs. We have to keep that part of the equation from her. If she suspects anything, not only will she hunt down Damaris but also anyone corrupt within Internal Affairs. I want to keep the second part of her mind. Let her concentrate on Damaris, let her think he's the only piece on the chessboard."

Donovan chuckles. "Damaris thinks he's at the top of this organization."

I laugh. "He can think what he wants. His hatred of his brother pushes him to make wrong decisions, which serves our cause. He's disposable and only thinks of himself. If he really were part of the cause, he'd never have gotten himself in the situation he's in. He's weak, but for now, he serves a purpose. I do need more high-ranking vampires in our group though so they can convince others to join us."

"I agree."

"Go, Donovan, keep him busy and make him think he's in charge. We know the truth. Give your mate my blessing."

Donovan smiles. "I will. I'll get back to him. He can't go outside at the moment. We've hidden him, but some of his goons have something for him, so we'll have to let him out tonight so he can pick it up."

"Good, remind him he needs to convince another vampire to join us. We need more than just the ones that are working for him."

He nods and leaves. We have to rush the plan, but we'll make it work. We will have a revolution and blood will be shed, but in the end, everything will go back to normal, and we'll be closer. No more factions, only us ruling at the top and humans at the bottom.

5. CASEY

KANE LEADS THE WAY AS WE ENTER THE conference room and Lizbeth screams and rushes toward me. "You're here."

I smile. "Yep, so I hope you're good. Do you need more blood and sleep than Kane can provide?"

I'm teasing her, and her cheeks start to color. She's over a hundred years old, but per what's standard behavior when a vampire falls in love, she's acting more like a human teenager.

"Stop! I'm not talking about that. So, do you have news on Damaris?"

"Not yet. I'm following some of his goons, and I'm sure they'll be meeting at a club. They have something to give Damaris."

"That's not good. Does Alto know?"

"Not that I'm aware."

I take a chair and wait for the rest of the team to arrive. Once they do and everyone is seated, Kane starts the meeting. "What do you need and what can we do to help?"

"I have two cases I need help with. Damaris has to be brought in alive so we can interrogate him and find out what's going on in the community for one. The other is not official, but I need to investigate my boss. I'm pretty sure something is up in Internal Affairs. Corruption is generally minimal because we're not blood-related to any of the factions and although He's a full vampire, his maker has been dead for a century so He's as close to being a daywalker as a full vampire can get."

"You mean with his maker dead, the blood call isn't as strong?" Kane asks me.

"Yes, well, that's what we thought, but I'm not sure anymore."

Lizbeth speaks up. "What makes you think something's happening?"

"Since I've been working for Internal Affairs, which as you know is a long time, my boss has never tried to stop an investigation. Now it's like he doesn't want me to find something. I need to contact someone inside. My closet colleagues can help if they haven't been corrupted, which I doubt they have."

"What makes you think that?" Kane asks.

"Daywalkers don't want power, we want justice. That's part of our blood. Usually, when we have a mission, we stick to it until we succeed or we die trying. My boss knows that he's been there longer than I have. That's why I don't understand why he wants me to quit this mission."

"Who are you going to contact?"

While we don't generally make friends or become close to each other because we never know if we'll die during a mission, I do have one friend there. "I think Jade will help if I ask her. I need a secure line to call her though. I don't want to be traced here. I can't guarantee she'll do it, but it's worth a shot."

Lizbeth looks into my eyes as if she's trying to see inside

my soul. "I agree. It's worth a try. Don't worry, we'll meet with Greg, and he'll be able to help you."

I nod. I hope I'm wrong about what's happening at Internal Affairs, but my gut tells me otherwise. I follow Kane to a door that's further away from all the others and He knocks.

"What?" a voice yells at us.

Kane chuckles and opens it. "We have a visitor, you know that, right? I hope you read the memo."

I'm surprised as I see Greg for the first time. I didn't think someone who was as big a geek as he was would be packed with muscle like he is. I think need to change my image of what a geek looks like.

He stands, and I see he's tall too. "Sorry, I'm in the middle of something. You must be Casey." He extends his hand, which I take, and we shake.

"Yes. I guess with the hacking thing you were able to find a picture of me."

He seriously blushes. "Maybe. What do you need? And yes, Kane, I read the fucking memo."

Kane laughs. I'm not sure I understand what's happening, but I let it go. I don't want to be involved in something I don't understand.

"I need a secure line that can't be traced back to here."

He points to an old phone. "Easy, use that phone there."

"You still have that antique?" Kane asks.

"Yes. That phone doesn't have GPS, and it's harder to trace."

I take it and dial.

"Vampire Internal Affairs, how can I help you?" I know the voice. It's Margaret, our general assistant, and receptionist.

"Can I speak to Jade, please?" I've known Jade since she was in what humans would call daycare.

"Yes, one moment, please." She puts me on hold.

"Jade speaking."

"Hey, Jade, it's Casey."

"Fuck, Casey. Why have you called?"

She's whispering so things must be worse there than I thought.

"I can't call a longtime colleague and friend?" I ask her, hoping to smooth things over a little.

"That's not it, and I'm guessing you know it. The boss is searching for you."

Oh, that's not good. "Are you in charge of finding me?" I cross my fingers, hoping she's not.

"No, none of us are. He can't force us. You know how it works. All of us know you're on a mission, and that's why you haven't been in the office."

I breathe a little easier. "Who's looking then?"

"We don't know them, but something's not right. Have you found that vampire yet?"

"No, Grant stopped me from doing any research. The SIA Investigation Team is helping me with information and resources that fucker cut me off from."

She laughs. "He's cut us off too, depending on which mission we're working on. We've been meeting outside the office to talk about things. We've had lots of visits from weird men."

"Vampires?" I ask.

"Some yes and some not. It changes every time. I could be nothing, but at the same time, it might not be. We've come to the conclusion the boss isn't impartial. You know what that means."

Fuck, that's something I didn't want her to confirm. "Can you do me a favor?"

"Sure, anything for you. You've saved my butt more times than I can count."

I smile. I mentored her when she first started. "Can you spy from the inside and report to me?"

There is silence on the phone for a couple of seconds. "Sure, how?"

I think. "You know the little cafe in the Old Port?"

"Your favorite one?"

I smile. "That's the one. Every Friday morning, we'll meet there. It's far enough from the office, and it's in the neutral zone."

"So it's Tuesday, that means we meet Friday this week?" she asks.

"Yes, if we feel the place is compromised, we'll find another one." I sigh. "That cafe belongs to a witch, an old one that's powerful enough to bring a lot of vampires to their knees and is less likely to be corrupted as well."

She laughs. "True. She could be mad for all we know," Jade says.

"I'll meet you on Friday at around nine in the morning."

"Fine, I'll be there."

"What's happened?"

I turn toward Kane. "Something is fishy at the bureau. Jade told me Grant has stopped some investigations, which he's not supposed to do. She will spy for us, and we'll meet each Friday morning, at a cafe that both of us know. It's owned by an ancient witch and she has a mind of her own."

"Casey, what else do you need?" Greg asks me.

Where to start. "Can you try to locate my boss and see where he's been and anyone he's met with for the past two weeks?"

"Now you've given me a challenge. I was hoping you'd need more than just a phone," Greg teases me.

I laugh at Greg, and Kane smiles at me.

"I'll leave you both to work. If you need me, Casey, Greg knows where to reach me." Kane heads to the door.

"Kane." He turns when I call his name. "Thanks, it means a lot to me."

"Don't worry about it, Casey. You helped me with Lizbeth, and she means the world to me. Catch Damaris, and I'll consider us even." With that, he disappears down the corridor.

"So, sweetheart, where do you want me to start?"

"I need to see what he's been doing outside office hours."

He starts to tap on his keyboard. "He's a vampire, right?"

I look on the screen and see a picture of him. "Yes, he is, but he's not part of any faction."

Greg doesn't look at me but continues his work. "Our database is limited, but I can hack yours if you give me your information." I give him my card and ID. "Don't worry, Casey, they won't be able to trace me."

I laugh. "Maybe, but just to be sure, I'll send a text to Jade. She's the one in charge of network security."

"You don't trust me?" Greg seems hurt.

"It's not that, but we don't need any red flags right now. She'll cover for us if needed at the network."

I watch Greg's fingers flying over the keyboard for a while. "Hmmm."

I look at him. "What?"

He jumps, it's almost as if he forgot I'm here. "Fuck, Casey, don't scare me like that. Let me work, I'll tell you as soon as I find something."

"OK. Can you tell me how to find Kane?"

"He's waiting for you outside the door. I sent him a text to pick you up."

The door opens. "Come on, Casey, leave the master to work on his masterpiece."

I follow Kane. "Show me the way." Kane smiles as I leave the office. "Is he always like this?"

Kane chuckles. "He can be worse. He's a great guy, but

there's a reason he's alone. That computer of his is his woman. I can't imagine any female wants to compete with that."

"If you say so. It's almost dark, and I need to follow those goons again. I'm pretty sure they're going to a club to take stuff to Damaris."

"Do you need back -up?"

"Nah, I'm good. You still have someone watching the restaurant?"

He nods.

"No activity whatsoever?"

"The last report I received no one had left."

"Ok, I'm heading back there. It's nearly night and knowing Damaris, he needs less sleep than your mate does. That could mean those goons could head there earlier."

"Need any equipment?" Kane asks.

"No, I have a hiding place for my stuff. Not even Internal Affairs knows about it. I'll go there first, then head to the border and wait."

Kane nods and shows me out. "Call if you need help. The door is always open for you. Keep me posted about everything."

"Yes, don't worry, I will. Make sure Greg contacts me if he finds something on his end."

I head to my hiding place. I need to be ready, it's almost night, and action is in the air.

6. DAMARIS

I HEAD TOWARD THE BLACK LOTUS. IT BELONGS to Jeremy, and it's where I'm going to meet my goons. He's interested in joining us and needs more information which I'll gladly provide. It also gives me a place to eat and fuck. My goons should arrive soon with my special package. I hope they have it. If they don't, I'll have to kill them.

We enter through the private parking lot and I'm in a limo with tinted glass thanks to Donovan. It means I can travel and don't have to worry about being seen. My driver opens the door after he makes sure the place is secure, and I see Jeremy waiting for me.

"Ah, Damaris, my friend."

"Thanks for helping me and having me as your guest."

Jeremy smiles in acknowledgment. We enter the elevator, and he presses the button for the top floor. The club is on the ground floor, so I'm guessing Jeremy wants to talk to me first.

"We have a few hours before the club opens. I think you need to eat and maybe indulge in some other pleasures." That's the life I want. Everyone at my service and to have any women I want.

"It's welcome. I need it."

The elevator doors open and I see it's given us direct access to the penthouse. "Come, we'll talk, and then I'll leave you with your meal." The windows are tightly closed and darkened—only a vampire would build something like this.

"What do you want to talk about?"

Jeremy smiles at me again and gets straight to the point. "What is this rebellion you've tried to create all about?"

"You know how our communities work. That needs to change. We all need the chance to have a better life, and not be ruled by the circumstances of our birth."

We sit side by side on the sofa and Jeremy looks at me. "What you want is to have a bigger piece of the pie, and in some ways, rule the community."

"It's more than that. More and more humans are finding out about us. Some of them want to join us, and they serve to be worthy. I know some of the shifters have started to mate outside their community. Their fated system isn't binding them to other shifters anymore. They're spending more time in the neutral zone as most of their mates can't go to their clans, especially witches or other paranormal creatures, but humans can. We want that stopped."

Jeremy laughs. "Oh, did you memorize that speech? You seem more like a salesman than the real you. I know you, Damaris. Your activities and motivations aren't that pure, and I'm guessing you've given that speech to a lot of people, but the reality is totally different. I don't know about the other factions, but for a vampire, blood and power are what we want. You can't bear that you've been ousted from power because Alto found his fated mate, which is something you don't have, and now he has someone to rule after he turns to dust."

I'm not shocked at his response, Jeremy is as wild as I am. "Fine, I'll cut the crap. The group I'm in thinks that.

Although I'm not totally sure it's what the leader is really planning, it's what the people that joined us want. You're right. You're in the same position I am. No access to power because our brothers have mated. I'm not here to sell you something. I want you to join us, not to sit around and sing kumbaya but so you can take control of your life for yourself."

Jeremy crosses his legs. "What do you really want, Damaris, from all this?"

"Simple. Power, blood, and to make my brother pay for what he did to me. He believes her instead of his brother. His son wants to be with me, for reasons I don't understand. I'm starting to think he wants to rule now and not wait for his father to turn to dust."

"I know you want blood, but do you want something stronger too?"

We can eat regular food, which could be why a lot of humans don't think we exist, but we can't live on that, we need blood to survive. "Yes, do you have any whiskey?"

He stands and goes to a small bar in the corner of the room before returning and handing me a drink and sitting again with his. I take a sip before getting back to our conversation. "So what do you think? You know you'll never be able to rule and will always have to follow your brother's rules."

Jeremy takes a drink before he speaks. "I see what you're doing. You're playing their game until you're satisfied and able to strike to obtain what you want."

"Guilty as charged. Don't tell me you've never thought about it. I know you did a century ago."

Jeremy winces at my statement. "That was a long time ago. I didn't succeed, and I was lucky my brother let me live, but I'm not sure that'll be the case this time if we don't succeed. At that time, he didn't have a son or a mate, and he needed to keep me alive to keep the bloodline strong."

"Now he has and what has he done? He's pushed you out

slowly but surely. You may need a few centuries, but after that, what'll happen? Especially if his son finds his mate and has a vampire born from himself. You know as well as I do that our chance to be in charge is growing smaller and smaller. We need to reverse that and build something new without the vampire monarchies."

Jeremy doesn't answer, and I can see he's deep in thought. Someone knocks at the door, bringing him back to the present. "Come in," he calls.

One of the bouncers enters with a young vampire. "Jeremy, you asked for her?" the bouncer says.

"Yes, leave us. Come, little one." She hesitates but compiles. "Sarah, this is my old friend Damaris. He needs your services tonight. Will you give that to him?"

She smiles at me. "Sure, he's handsome."

I chuckle as Jeremy stands. "We'll talk later, my friend, but yes, your proposition is exciting. I'll leave you to your meal, and we'll talk again after. Sarah, you know the rules, satisfy him in any way he requires." She nods at Jeremy. "When your goons arrive, I'll let you know, but until then you have a couple of hours with her. No one will disturb you."

He closes the door, and my mouth starts to water. "Sarah, you're a young vampire. How old are you?"

She comes closer to me. "I've been a vampire for twenty-five years."

I stroke her cheek. "A baby in the vampire world. Come and kiss me."

She moves closer and my dick hardens as her small form sits on my lap. "Sure, I can do that, sir."

Her lips come to mine. My hand goes to her tits, which are round and full. Her nipples peak at my touch. I stop the kiss and put her over my shoulder and head toward the bedroom.

"Now, my little one, you will have sex and blood like you've never had it before."

She mewls at this. I remove my clothes, and she does the same. Both of us are naked, her eyes are red with lust like mine should be. Our fangs are out to play too. I grab behind her head. "You are willing to give me sex and your blood?"

She licks her lips, the bitch turns me on. It's been a while since I've had a little vampire so willing. "Yes, sir, I give it freely to you."

I kiss her hard, my finger lands on her pussy at the same time. I need it all, hard and fast. She undulates against me. She's small, and I'm big, but since she's a vampire I have no problem being rough as I know she can take it. I stop kissing her, and my mouth goes to her clit, and I start to suck and lick it.

"Please, sir."

"Begging, my little one? Tell me what you want?"

"Your cock inside me and your fangs at my vein to drink my blood."

I smile. "So sweet like your taste. I will grant your request."

I align my cock to her entrance and slam inside her. She screams with pain and pleasure. Her tits bounce each time I thrust inside her. I want hard and fast, I've no time for more.

"More, sir."

"You want more, little girl? I will give it to you."

Not only can we run fast, but we can fuck fast. I increase my pace, and she screams her release, but I want more, need more. Her blood calls to me. I know she's not my mate, but she's good enough to eat and fuck. I'm close to coming, but I need her blood. I push her head to the side until I see her vein and lick the spot between her neck and shoulder. My fangs are ready to drink, and both of us are ready to come. I bite hard and tap her blood. She screams and comes again, and I do the same. Lucky for us a vampire can only breed with their mate. I don't have to put on a condom or have anything between us.

I release her neck and lick the wound before heading to the bathroom.

"Sir?"

I smile at her. "That was great. You need to clean up, and I have a meeting soon. We can have round two later."

She jumps from the bed and heads to the bathroom. The shower is big enough for us to fuck again. I slap her butt and push her against the wall. I've changed my mind, and I'm ready for round two now. I don't know when I'll have another one like her.

7. CASEY

AS SOON AS I ARRIVE AT MY HIDING PLACE, I load my stuff. I take my katana and guns along with extra ammunition. I look at my katana, there are so many memories associated with it. It's been two hundred years since I was born. My mother was pregnant, and a young vampire drank her blood, which killed her, but there was enough time for me to be safely born before she died from the loss of blood.

I grew up in a small village. A couple that couldn't have children took me in. During that time, I was happy and thought I was human, although I knew something was different about me. I slept less than my parents and ate less too. I was strong, but most of the time I hid it. They had seen it once, and from the way, people looked at me after, I knew I made them uneasy until another vampire came to our town and started to attack the village and tried to kill everyone in it. I was sixteen at the time. I was able to take that young vampire with my bare hands and save the village but not my parents. If before they weren't sure about me, afterward they almost worshiped me. I wasn't used to that much attention. Since nothing held me there, I decide to travel, which took me to Japan, where I stayed for fifty years.

I was lucky. At that time, women weren't allowed to learn how to fight in any way. Sensei saw things differently, he knew what and who I was. Memories of a long past conversation flood my mind.

"Casey."

I bow my head. "Yes, Sensei?"

"Come, I need to show you something."

I follow him, and we head to the forbidden cave, the place only a Sensei can go. I stop just in front of it, unsure of myself.

"Come, child." I follow him, and he turns and looks at me. "You're wondering why we're here?"

I nod, not having to say anything.

"Casey, you're special in ways you don't know yet. You wonder about your life, why you're different from others, why you're faster, stronger, and need less sleep. I know you also need blood but just a little."

I don't reply but wait for him to continue.

"I know what you are. You said your mother was killed and that you were saved just in time, and a couple took you in. You also told me how you left your village because it was attacked by a creature the people in your village called a bloodsucker."

He sits on the ground, and I follow him. The night is almost here. "There are a lot of things we don't understand in life, and it will probably be a century or more before humans do."

"Did you say, humans, Sensei?"

He smiles at me. "You're human, but you've been elevated, the same way I have." I absorb what Sensei is saying. "Yes, Casey, I'm like you. That's one of the reasons I decided to teach you when women aren't allowed to learn. The creature that killed your parents and made you the way you are is called a vampire."

"Vampire?"

"Yes, they're a creature that drinks blood and kills without mercy.

I've done some research, and they do have weaknesses. One of the things I've discovered is that they can't be out in the sun as it kills them. I was able to capture one once, and I didn't know about the sun. As soon we went outside, he started to scream and turned to dust in front of my eyes. Not only that, my mother had the same fate as yours. We are more similar than you know, my little one."

My Sensei stops talking, and I have so many questions. "Wait, we are?"

He sighs. "We are called daywalkers since those creatures called vampires can't go outside during daylight. We have the same structure as them, but we're immune to the sun. We can eat food like a regular human, but sometimes we need blood. Especially if we are wounded or need to replenish our stamina. We can run faster, are stronger, and we have the ability to take a hit and heal faster. That's another of the reasons I agreed to teach you. I knew you needed to be able to defend yourself. A lot of my students came to me after I decided to help you say it wasn't acceptable. Some even left to go to another temple. I stand by my position, for the reasons I told you. You need to be trained so you can be ready for anything."

It was too much, why has this happened to me? "Sensei, why did he choose my mother?"

He takes my hand. "Child, they never choose, it just happened that your mother was there. The vampire doesn't understand us, although one day maybe he will. I believe my mother died from the same vampire yours did. You were fortunate like I was. Someone took the chance and saved you even if your mother was almost dead."

"Why now? Why tell me now?"

The Sensei comes closer and puts his hand on my shoulder. "It's been a few years now, and it is time for you to start your journey. My research leads me to believe that most of the vampires have decided to go to the new colony. You have space, and who knows what will happen there. You need to control the vampires. They can't invade there the same way they did here and other countries."

I look at him then. I've been training for a few years with him. "But I'm not fully trained."

He smiles at me. "You're more than ready. You manipulate the katana like none of my other students do. You will grow and continue your training by yourself. You need to do this."

"You've had a vision?" I know he has them occasionally.

"Yes, my vision tells me you need to go to Canada, more specifically to a town called Montreal. You have a great future in front of you, and a lot of people need you. You may not know it yet, but one day, you will understand."

I close my eyes at the memory. It's been years since I've thought about Sensei. Usually, when that happens, something is coming, and the community needs me. I miss him, he was taken by surprise and was killed by a young vampire. I'm grateful for what he taught me, though. Without him, I don't know how I would have survived those years.

I look in the mirror. I'm ready, but I don't know what will happen at the club.

Reaching the restaurant, I position myself as close as I can, see some of Kane's men also watching and head over to them. "So, no one has left yet?"

One of the men jumps. "Fuck, they told us you're like a ninja but I didn't believe them. I never heard you coming."

I smile. Being a daywalker gives me a lot of advantages from humans but also other paranormal creatures inside the community. "Don't worry, you're not the first and won't be the last."

"No one..." the second man starts to say, but I tune him out when I see the goons leave the restaurant. They have a package and take a taxi.

"Great, boys. Now go back to Kane and I'll let Greg know. You can follow from there."

"Kane told us to stay with you."

That big alpha badass is obviously trying to protect me—

not that I need it. "You won't be able to follow me, I move too fast. You're better staying at HQ until I need back -up." With that, I start to run. The night is almost here, and I need to be careful because people could see me. I follow the goons to The Black Lotus, Jeremy Thompson's club, and see Damaris's goons approaching which confirms Damaris is here.

They head to the back of the building as the club isn't open yet. I put myself close enough to listen.

A big bouncer appears after opening the door. "What do you want?"

"We are here for my master." The main goon shows him something. That could be his mark.

"Fine, come inside."

I need a plan to get inside. This is a high-end club, and since we are in downtown Montreal, it doesn't have windows that open like the buildings in the Old Port do. The building isn't that tall, I may be able to find a way to breach it from the roof. It's child's play to pick a lock. The night is coming though, and if I break in dressed like this, I'll be easily spotted.

Entering through the front door is my best bet. My phone buzzes. "Casey."

"You find anything?"

"Hey, Jade. Yes, but I'm still working on it, and you?"

"It's not good news. I called because something is going to happen tonight. I heard the boss say he needs to go to The Black Lotus. It's a club in downtown."

"What?"

"Yes, he said he has to meet someone there."

"Do you know who he was talking to?"

"Someone on the phone. I was passing his office, and the door was open. He also stopped Sophia's mission. She disappeared just after you did. I know she's still doing her mission."

The whole thing smells fishy. "What do you think is happening, Jade?"

"Good question. I'm not on a mission, but I wonder if it will happen to me too. There is definitely something going on with Grant."

I pinch my nose. "Jade, I'm outside the same club. Damaris's goons are here as well."

"*Fuck*. You don't think he's meeting him, do you?"

I stay silent.

"Yes, you're right. *Shit.* isn't he supposed to be impartial?"

"Yes, he is, but obviously, he isn't."

"Why is he the boss then?"

"You know why, I've already told you that. The head of each family in the faction wanted to have one of their own in charge, but that wouldn't have given them balance. He was the best choice, as without a blood allegiance to anyone he's not supposed to be swayed by any of the factions. He's like us, only a full vampire. That's why our office is underground. It gives the vampire community peace of mind since as per them, it's in balance. Now we know that's not the case."

Jade didn't say anything. "What next?"

"I have to get inside, but you know how the club is. I think the best thing to do is the enter by the front door. For that, I need a dress, my weapons hidden, and on top of that, clearance or an invitation."

Most of the clubs allow anyone access, but a few are more select. Unfortunately, this was one of those.

"I'm guessing you have weapons but not the rest."

Most female daywalkers love to wear dresses, and we certainly have the body for it. I've never enjoyed it, though. More often than not, a dress is in my way when I need to fight someone. "Bullseye. How did you know?" I tease her.

She laughs. "Fine, come to my place. it will be dark soon,

and the club opens an hour after sunset. I'll see what I can do to secure an invitation."

"Thanks, Jade, I owe you one."

"Yeah, I know, and I'll try to keep a low profile at the office, just in case."

"I'll meet you at your place. I'll come around the back to your balcony."

"OK. I'm leaving now. See you soon. Bye."

She hangs up. The plan has changed. She'd better have a dress that I can fight in and carry my weapons. *Oh crap, I'll have to wear fucking high heels as well.*

8. THE LADY

SOMEWHERE ON THE TOP OF THE MOST PROMINENT building.

"MY LADY."

I look at my personal assistant. "Yes, Selena?"

She sits in front of me. "We have more news from the Internal Affairs office."

"What is it?"

She takes a deep breath. "Some of the daywalkers have gone rogue. Some haven't reported for days or weeks, and they're on missions that could bring them close to us. From what I understand, the head of Internal Affairs is supposed to be meeting with Damaris later tonight."

I stand and look through the window. "Which of the daywalkers are missing?"

"We know that Casey, Sophia, and Jess are reported as not having been to the office in a couple of weeks, and he doesn't know where they are. We don't know where they are either."

It's that fucking Damaris's fault. "We know where Casey is, have we been able to locate the others?"

"No, we've tried."

"Any news from the other factions?"

"We know the witches are also working with the Investigation Team, but nothing more than that. It's hard to get information from the witches."

My assistant is right, the witches can be a pain in the ass. "Have you contacted the dark one from the witches?"

"We did, my Lady. Some will join us, but the strongest ones are not on the dark side of magic. Physically, the warrior witches are the strongest and are revered by the other witches. We need to corrupt them while they're young. We can do that with Paranormal University students."

"No, we can't. My agreement with Gorad is simple. He wants the university for himself. I agree with him. We stick with the factions. We need more witches corrupted to our cause, but also fae, demons, and any other creatures that exist in our community. We need to make them see. We also need more vampires. They may be bloodsuckers, but we need their money and influence."

I look through the window to see night has fallen, and the community is starting to come alive, but I want more than that. Humans will know us, we will be the ones at the top of the power chain. They need to know that for the most part they either mate or kowtow to us. That fucking Damaris needs to know his place. I need him, but at the same time, I'll be glad to kill him myself. We may have been able to corrupt the boss at the vampire Internal Affairs, but I need some daywalkers. Like the warrior witches, they are hard to corrupt. "So, where is our team right now?"

"We have a team going after Solomon's Seal. From our research, we also need the Stone of Destiny. We have others on the list too, but we only have a few teams for those missions."

I start to pace. We need to gather more people to our cause, or it will slow down. Now that we need to deal with Damaris, which could bring attention to us, things are getting messy. "How is recruitment going?"

"It's a little more difficult since we need to cover Damaris. We have two teams that can gather objects, the third is busy on his case, the fourth is the one that can do the corrupting, but we need more, my Lady. Now that we need to rush our plan, we need followers to go on missions and gather the artifacts we need to succeed."

I know all this. I know the plan and how it will work. The Damaris situation doesn't help us, we need fewer eyes looking for us, not more. We need to be back underground and fast. "What do you suggest?"

"We need to start talking with the fae, some of them might be easier to convince. We also need more demons, if not half-demons."

"You know what happens to half-demons if they go down the dark path, they became full demons. Their human side will be completely swallowed by their demon side, but you're right. We need more people to join our cause."

It's that simple, we need more people to join our ranks. We need to push our plan faster so that we can be victorious.

"I know, but we need people to talk with others who can be corrupted. At the same time, maybe them finding out about us is better and faster. It could work to our advantage and start to spread things about us that could make people change their focus and join us willingly."

"You may be right. We've been in hiding for so long, and we are progressing but not the way I want it. We wanted to go slow to have solid ground, but now we need to speed up. Who will connect with the fae?" I ask.

"Don't worry, my cousin married one, and they are against the system as it sounds. He told me that black ones exist. It's something we can investigate. They might be hard to corrupt to join our cause, but we can try."

We started with a few seeds of this rebellion, now it's time to spread and grow. "That's good, we'll start there. I know that the lower classes in each faction have a reason to join our cause. Their fate is doomed, even before it starts. The system needs to change, everyone has the right to be on top." I want to be over all of them. I need to be the supreme of all. some way, the people of my past will pay for what they did to me when they exiled me in my own land.

"Do it. Make the necessary arrangements to let our troops know that we're recruiting on a large scale, and we need more teams for the missions. It's taking too long to find the artifacts and the warrior witches are working against us. The order is simple. Kill them if they get in the way. No excuses."

"Excellent, my Lady, I will let our group leader know. I think they'll like it a lot."

I nod, they've pushed me to take this route, so be it. The end justifies the means. The door closes, but I don't look back. I know I'm alone in my room and can let my guard down as I look through the window. The system needs to crash, every time in history men try to change things, a rebellion is needed to achieve it. Well, so be it. the rebellion starts tonight, and we will not only recruit, but we will hit harder than we have so far. Every rebellion brings bloodshed, so let's have a blood rebellion that will be the end of this system that doesn't work and put me back where I should've been, and everyone that was involved in my removal will pay.

---

9. CASEY

I'M AT JADE'S APARTMENT, AND FOR THE LAST HOUR, she's made me try on dress after dress. Ah, fuck, I hate it. I need a dress that not only hides my guns but my katana too— with my long red hair, I'm noticeable.

"We'll need to put your hair up so you don't attract too much attention. Not only that, you need to be able to see clearly. A lot of people attend these parties."

I smile at her. "Thank goodness you were able to secure me an invitation."

"It's fake, so let's hope they don't look at it too hard. And don't ask how I got it because I'm not telling."

I laugh but don't ask any more questions. A daywalker never judges how another daywalker works. We all understand that sometimes extreme measures are needed to succeed in our missions.

"Put this on." She gives me a short skirt, but it's not too tight against my body. It's black, and I pair it with a white blouse and put a black jacket with it.

"You really don't like me, do you, Jade? Why that skirt?"

She laughs. "I'll always love you like a sister, Casey. You'll be able to hide your guns with that skirt since it's less tight."

"And my katana?"

"No, you won't be able to take your katana. We can't hide it. If it were a Halloween party, then it would be easy, but it isn't. Just so you know, these parties can get pretty wild."

I cross my arms. "You seem to know a lot for a person that's never put a foot inside there."

Her cheeks turn red. "I didn't say that, Casey. You just assumed I've never been there."

"You've been? And not just once, right?"

"Yes. I went as part of a job the first time, but I've been since for pleasure too. Especially when I need blood. Which as you know isn't too often."

I'm stunned, and it takes me a minute to find my voice. "You've done it? You've bitten someone like a vampire does?"

She gets redder but doesn't say anything.

"You have blood here. Why do you need to go to a club for it?"

Jade starts to put the clothing I rejected in the closet. "The first time was an accident. Not only can you find blood there, but also sex."

I look at her, shocked. "Don't tell me he was a vampire?"

"No, he was a shifter, a werewolf to be precise. We fucked, and the temptation was too high."

A daywalker is like everyone else for the most part, but our impulses aren't as strong, or that's what I'd always thought. "Do you think other daywalkers have done it? Am I'm the only one that never has?"

Jade sighs. "You know that some of us have regular sex and even try to maintain a relationship. If you're talking about drinking blood from somebody else, I don't know. You know that's a taboo subject. I suspect some have, but I can't confirm it. Don't judge me. I've only told you because we've been friends for so long."

"Sorry, Jade, I'm shocked. Actually, I'm more than shocked. I didn't think we had that impulse." I start to play with the fabric of the skirt.

"Ask me, Casey. I know you well enough to see that you're dying to ask the question."

I look out her window. The night is there, and the club door opens in two hours. "What's it like?" I can't believe I'm asking her that. I've never been attracted enough to anyone to be tempted to drink their blood during sex. I'm always afraid of losing control.

"Do you mean the sex, or blood with sex?"

I'm confused, but at the same time curious. "What do you think? All of it?"

"Obviously the sex is great, but with the power of blood, multiply it by a thousand. It's almost addictive. Not the blood but the rush that comes with it."

I've had sex a few times, but it's always left me with a bitter taste in my mouth. This is why I don't do it often—only when my body craves it, and I can't control it anymore.

"Your brain is working hard, Casey. You can ask me anything."

"I'd never judge you, Jade. I'm surprised, that's all. I know we have needs, but it didn't occur to me you'd hook up with the same guy more than once."

She smiles, almost daydreaming. "Well, he said I'm his mate, which I didn't think was possible. He said his wolf howls inside his head every time he thinks of me. He wants to be with me all the time and fuck me. He doesn't mind that I'm a daywalker. At first, he thought I was a vampire. He likes that I can be out during daylight."

"How long have you been seeing him?"

"Five years."

"*Five years*? And you never told me?"

Jade is a badass daywalker, we all are. She's never kept a

secret like this from me.

"I know what you're thinking. I wasn't sure, to begin with. I thought I'd try and see what happened. I thought after a few months he'd be bored with me, but it never happened. I feel more alive when he's around me. Desire and love are there, and it's growing. I know we don't have anything that says we can't mate, and we assumed it wasn't possible. I'm proof it is."

"Ok, are you telling me he marked you? You don't have his mark."

"I do, but not everyone can see it. His wolf pack knows I belong to him. That's part of the mating—the smell his mark leaves on me."

If someone had told me my world would be rocked to its core these past few weeks, I would've laughed in their face. Damaris's case has revealed something far deeper and darker is going on in the community. My boss is acting weird, I'm working with the Investigation Team on a mission, other daywalkers have also gone rogue, and now I've discovered that we have the ability to mate.

Things are starting to change, and I'm not sure if it's a good thing. There are forces at work that we still don't understand.

"Are you mad?"

I look at my friend. "No. I wish I'd known earlier, but no, I'm not mad. As I said, I'm just surprised. Shocked is another word I'd use."

She smiles. "I know. I always wanted you to be the first to know. You know we don't have friends. At first, I fought it, and I even hit him. For him, he knew right away and wouldn't leave me alone. I will say my thirst increased with him around. Other blood didn't appeal to me, that's how I knew."

"Tell me, was it at a party like the one tonight where you found him?"

She blushes. "Yes, and no. As I said, the first time I went, it was part of a mission, and when I did, I saw everyone there. I'd never imagined different kinds of species could be in the same room and not kill each other. Not only that, some were mated and others were talking and interacting like they were friends. Then I saw Lucas with a fae, and I knew it wasn't a normal party."

"Lucas? He's been missing for a while now. I guess he's gone rogue."

"From what I understand, he mated that fae. He was on a mission that involved a rogue vampire killing fae. We didn't discuss his mission or anything. We all know we can be away from headquarters for days, if not weeks. Then I saw footage of him killing a werewolf. I'm guessing the werewolf was trying to kill his mate. It was around then I started to suspect something weird was going on with the boss, so I didn't report it. I know if she's his mate, his only mission was and is to protect her. His mate is his top priority. I'd be the same if something happened to Dean. It seems to be a basic instinct for us. Nothing is important if our mate isn't there. I destroyed the evidence to give him time to settle things and maybe work with us."

She starts doing my hair.

"Don't tell me he met her at that kind of party?"

She didn't say anything. "As far as I know, yes, he did. Having a place where rank and the differences between the species can be overlooked seems to help. Our guard drops, and we can be ourselves."

She finishes with my hair. I've never seen myself like this. "Do you think it's a bit over the top?"

"No, Casey, you will see."

"Are you telling me, Jade, that you believe something magical happens at those parties and it will happen to me as well?"

She comes in front of me and looks me directly in my eyes. "Go with an open mind. You have your mission, and I know that Damaris has to be taken down, but I think what he's possibly aiming for could be good if we want peace between everyone. A lot of us are tired of these centuries-long feuds that no one remembers or cares about how they started."

I didn't reply to her statement straight away. True, there are not only feuds between species but between the different factions and clans within species. "Maybe some of it could be good, but I feel in my blood there's an evil force behind it, and that force will be the end of us all."

She hands me my guns with a band that I can strap around each of my thighs. They're small in comparison to my usual ones, but I know they're powerful and can't be seen under the skirt.

"OK, let's see that invitation." She surprises me again when she shows me two tickets. "Why two?"

She smiles and heads into her walk-in wardrobe. "You didn't think I'd let you go alone, did you? Also, my mate will be there, which means I need to be there too since his pack knows about us and will wonder where I am."

"Really?"

"Yep, don't worry, he doesn't know about your mission. I told him I wanted him to meet my best friend."

I roll my eyes. "You'll behave?"

"I will if Damaris doesn't put himself in my path."

I laugh. "Don't worry, he'll be too busy dealing with me."

Now my curiosity is awake, and I wonder what these parties are like. I look at Jade getting ready and deep inside, I'm a little envious. I now know everyone has the ability to find a mate, including me, and that stirs something deep inside.

10. DAMARIS

THE LITTLE DISTRACTION JEREMY GAVE ME WAS worth it. My energy is back, and my balls are empty. "Enter!" I respond at a knock.

I watch the door open, and Jeremy comes in. "Well, I see that's done wonders for you." I smile in response. With Jeremy, you always get the best of everything. "Now that you've replenished yourself, the club won't open for another hour, so we have a bit of time to discuss your plans and all that comes with it." Jeremy sits on the couch and invites me to sit in front of him.

"You know how each faction works, and you know we can't do more than we are now. You're in the same position I am, except you're not being hunted down."

"True, we can't become the head of our family because we're too far from it for different reasons, and you think being a part of this rebellion is the way to change things?" Jeremy asks.

"Yes and no. What we want is freedom, that the neutral zone extends into each faction's territory. We're not the only ones who want that. We have some of the faes with us too. I know we're trying to gather as many followers as we can. We also need to gather some magical objects to help our quest." I want him to join me in the vampire faction. He's the only one I've considered a friend for over a century.

"Who's in charge?"

"I don't know much about her. I deal with Donovan. I know he calls her 'Lady'. She's in a position to give us what we both want."

"You're partnering with a dog now?"

"Stop. Donovan's never done anything to us. Yes, he is a dog, but we're working together to get what we want. He's mated to a witch. While it's not strictly forbidden, it's made them outcasts. None of us like that, and I think the Lady is an outcast from her faction as well. For me, I've had enough. I've already compromised myself with Alto. I'm his blood brother, but I'm also a threat to his family. You know that blood is sacred."

Jeremy crosses his long legs. "It's intriguing. I'm not surprised we aren't the only ones interested in seeing change."

I smile, I knew he'd be interested. "True, we're not the only ones not happy with the system. It needs a rebellion to force a change. If not, we'll be stuck with how things are for eternity."

"So you want a revolution?"

"Not a revolution but a rebellion, or more specifically a blood rebellion."

Jeremy doesn't reply and I can see he's thinking over what I said. "You know we'll lose a lot of our own in the process."

"That's a possibility, but don't forget that happens with every rebellion or revolution and after we will have the peace that we want. We need to clear the old blood and bring in new, but yes, the process will cost us at some point. That's a part of life."

"You're prepared to pay that cost?"

"You think that it hasn't cost me already? Not only is Casey from Internal Affairs looking for me but my brother is as well. I've committed treason, and I know it, but I'd rather take the chance for a better life for me and for us. You've always been my best friend. We're in the same situation. You'll never be able to rule over your brother's clan, that fucker has too many children to succeed him. You've been a puppet all these centuries, and you know you're worth more than that, as am I."

Jeremy stands and starts pacing. I let him think. I did the same the first time Donovan came to me. I'd never considered betraying my blood brother, but Donovan made me see things differently. He made me realize that my immortal life could be better, but we'd have to risk everything, to begin with. Yes, I've killed, but I've killed for the cause. I missed the opportunity to kill Lizbeth, but she'll be dead soon enough. Her half-demon mate will not stop me. She will die. That bitch was the start of my fall and caused me to lose my cover at the same time.

"What will you do if they capture you and try to take you back to Alto?"

"You know the rules in the neutral zone prevent them from handing me over even if they do capture me." I look around the penthouse and realize I've never asked Jeremy about his club. "Speaking of family, I've always wondered why you have this club separate from yours. You're the only one in the vampire faction that has something like this."

He smiles at me. "Well, it's something my father worked for, but he also told me that one day he hoped we could have more like this place and not only in the neutral zone. He had a vision, but he never shared it with the rest of the family, only with me. My father believed that for all the species in the community to survive we needed to come together. I can see it's starting to happen. Some of us are starting to find our fated mates outside our own community and even within the human world. Your brother is a good example. His mate is human even though she was able to extend her life with his blood, but nonetheless, if his fated mate is killed, he will kill himself after he kills the one who did it."

True, I've been a witness to it for the last few decades. It started as a rare case, but now it's different. "I know vampires can turn humans, but they'll never be able to become high ranking. Only those that are born or mated to one can. They only have them for their blood and to fuck them. For other species, you need to born one to be one. We have the advantage, but now those in power are stopping us from turning people into vampires. They don't want the bloodlines tainted."

"And you think a rebellion will allow us all to become equal?"

"Most of the wars between us or with other factions have been going on for centuries, and most of us don't know what started them. They've become tales parents tell their young children to make them afraid or angry, to keep the war alive. I'll say for my part I'm doing it for selfish reasons as I want my brother out. I'm fucking tired of being his puppet. I'm doing it for myself first and if others benefit from it, so be it, but that's not my main goal."

Jeremy stops pacing and stands in front of me. He's the only person I know that can help me, and I can help him too. "What do you want from me?"

"Simple. I want you with me. We've fought wars before, and we watch each other's backs. We need a place like this for all the species to meet and maybe mate and fuck. You can provide that and blood for those that are in need. I need your expertise in those areas."

"If I agree, what's next?"

"We meet with Donovan. He knows the Lady and will put us in contact with her. I've met her once, but I've never seen her."

"Really? How do you know it's not a guy?"

I laugh. "I saw her shadow on the curtains, and I can tell she's got tits."

Jeremy smiles. "Only you, my friend, would say something like that. From what you've said, and for what my father wished it was, I'll jump with you. You're right, doing this forever isn't a life. I'll die from boredom. Contact Donovan and we can talk. I want to learn what he has to offer because I'm guessing we have more to give to him than he can give us."

"Fair enough." I take out my phone and dial Donovan. "It's me. Jeremy wants more details, he's interested in helping us...Yes, we are... No, nothing official, he just wants more information... Don't worry, we can make an exception for you and your mate... Yeah, you know the place. I'll let Jeremy know. See you later."

Jeremy stands. "I need to be downstairs, the party is starting, and I need to check on my guests."

I nod. "Donovan is coming, you need to tell your bouncer about him and his mate. He's the initial contact within the group. We'll talk later, but for now, let's go make the party fantastic."

Jeremy smiles at me. "Well, my friend, a party it will be. We need to have some fun before we talk more about business."

He smacks my back, and with that, we leave my room and head down for the private party. Jeremy runs the type of parties where you can meet all kinds of people. Some are mated, and it's the only place they can be with their mates.

We hear the beat of the music. The party has started, and we're going to have fun.

Will Jeremy join us? I'm afraid he already knows too much. If he doesn't agree to join us, the worst will happen, and he'll be killed. So tonight we party like tomorrow doesn't exist.

11. CASEY

"DO WE HAVE TO WAIT LONG?" IT'S CROWDED, AND the lineup is long.

"We've started to move, be patient. I'm telling you tonight will be worth it, and you know Damaris is here, so that doubles the prize," Jade tells me.

"I wasn't gifted with patience when I was born. I think she had a hangover that day and missed my birth." We can hear the beat of the music, the closer we get to the main entrance. A couple ahead of us starts to make out and I'm glad Jade told me what to expect with this party so I'm not shocked. I'll stay close to her, but I know at some point I'll have to explore by myself. We finally reach the front of the line, and a big bouncer stops us.

"Do you have invitations?" he asks, and I look at Jade expecting her to pull them out.

"I'm Dean's mate. He said I could bring a friend tonight."

The bouncer starts to smell Jade, obviously confirming her story. "Dean is already here. He told me about his mate, but I didn't know she was a daywalker."

"You never know who your fated mate is going to be," she replies.

"Your friend has a name?"

"I'm Cas..." I start to say when Jade hits me. Not that I want to give my real name, but with the mission, the less that people who know it, the better.

He winks me. "Nice to meet you, Cass. Maybe we can meet later."

That's weird. "Sure."

With that, he lets us enter. I'll never understand the whole flirting thing. "Jade, how come you didn't use the fake invitations?"

She looks at me. "They were my backup plan, in case that didn't work. It's lucky he thought you were attractive." She laughs, and I roll my eyes.

She takes my hand, and we head to the back of the room, passing the dance floor where people are dancing, or rather rubbing against each other. Others have private booths and are talking, kissing, or fucking which makes my eyes widen just a little. I can see so many different kinds of people, not only different species but different clans within their factions.

Jade screams and jumps on a male, and I guess it's her mate. She kisses him full on the mouth. I never really think about sex and love The combination has always been taboo in my mind. We've been taught that love doesn't exist for us and that's why we're perfect for doing the job we're trained to do. Not only that, because we're not blood-related to any family, it means we're impartial when it comes to the factions.

"Love, this is my best friend Casey, but if anyone asks, tonight her name is Cass. I'll explain why later."

He nods and kisses Jade on her cheek, then extends his hand to me without releasing Jade. I shake it. "Nice to meet you. I've heard a lot about you."

"Likewise. Jade's told me much about you as well. I was

hoping when she decided to bring me here, I'd get to meet you."

"Jade told you about us?"

I nod.

"Good. It's good you finally know even daywalkers can have a fated mate. I know a few that have them."

I thought Jade was the only one who'd found a mate but from what he said there's more of us that have mated. I'm curious now wondering Who else at Internal Affairs has found a mate since that's where all the daywalkers work. "They told us differently."

"I know, but it's bullshit. You never know when you're going to find your mate. I'm just unhappy we can't live together. I hope one day that will change."

"Hey, Dean, long time no see."

Our conversation is interrupted as a group of people come and shake Dean's hand.

Jade gets up from her mate's lap to sit close to me. "What did I tell you?"

I need to process everything. If it's true, it will change all kinds of parameters inside Internal Affairs and also the factions.

"A lot of people know?" I ask in her ear.

"Only people that come here, and they don't talk. It's one of the rules."

I have some serious thinking to do after tonight. "I need to go to the washroom, where is it?" I ask Jade.

She points me in the right direction. "Don't be too long or you'll bring unwanted attention."

I agree and see her whispering to her mate. He nods at me. Jade knows I'm on a mission, but it's also an eye-opener. Has Internal Affairs kept us in the dark for a specific reason? Why has no one never told us? The more I think, the more questions it brings. Now is not the right time to be thinking about it. I need to focus on why I'm here.

Once I finish in the bathroom, I look around and scout the surroundings. I pass beside the dance floor again as I head back to Jade and her mate. Jade knows I love to dance, but not tonight. Maybe another time.

"Hey, come here. Dance with me." Someone grabs me from behind and slams me against him. The smell is disgusting, and his big hands start to roam over my body. I feel sick. I've never been in this position before, and I freeze. I know how to fight, but I've never been groped before.

I'm suddenly released and turn around when I hear someone groaning behind me to see a man lying on the floor.

"Do not touch her." A large werewolf male with short black hair and lots of muscles on display is standing over a man.

"She's unmated, she's fair game." Now that I can see my attacker, I realize he's a bear shifter. No wonder he smelled.

"She's mine. If you don't back off, I will kill you."

"Whoa there, I don't belong to anyone."

My savior kicks the bear shifter and grabs my hand, pulling me along as he leaves the dance floor. His touch stops me from retaliating against him. I'm surprised to discover that his growling, along with him grabbing my hand in his strong grip, has made my pussy wet and ready. I see Jade start to stand, but her mate stops her. Her mouth opens and closes as Dean whispers to her, and shock widens her eyes.

"Hey! I'm not your mate, and where are you taking me?"

Without saying anything, he grabs me and puts me over his shoulder, and I suddenly know how a potato sack feels. I start to hit his butt, which is hot under my hand. He enters a room and turns on the light before putting me down and locking the door.

"What's the meaning of all this?"

I'm finally able to see his face. Along with his short black hair, he has blue eyes, which turn bright yellow then blue again. I guess he's fighting his wolf right now. I start to walk backward until I hit a desk, telling me this is some kind of office.

His breath is raging, and he steps closer. "You're a daywalker?"

I suck in a breath at his voice. Why is my fucking body reacting like this, and why aren't I fighting him? "Yes, I am."

"I know what you're thinking, and the answer is simple. Your body is reacting to me because you're my fated mate."

I chuckle. "Really? Not true. I don't feel anything for you, no desire whatsoever." I try to get some distance between us. I don't know him, and I don't trust him.

He smiles, and I can see his werewolf fangs showing a little. "Now I know you're lying. Tell me, why aren't you fighting me? I know you're able to easily free yourself. If I touch you, you're going to melt."

"Dream on."

"I'd rather have the real deal versus a dream. You can't lie about your desire for me. I can smell that pussy of yours, and she knows her mate. I'm the only one that'll be able to drive you crazy with lust, and you'll beg me to fuck you."

For some reason, my body no longer belongs to me. Daywalkers smell delicious when we're aroused according to what I've been told in the past. My breath rages as He approaches me. It's the first time in my life I've felt like I'm the prey instead of the predator.

"If I let my beast out, you'd be on the floor, and I'll be mating you, marking you as mine. You know you want this. Your head can fight it, but your body craves it."

"We can't. I need to find someone. It's important that I track him down."

Despite my words, my body is on fire and only wants him

to move closer and play with it. I know in my head that I've got to catch Damaris, it's the only lead I've had for weeks.

He approaches me and looks in my eyes. "I know you're not lying and you'll need to help me understand, but I have to mark you. My wolf wants it, and so do I. It doesn't sit well with him that you're chasing another male."

I smile. damn werewolf, and for them, the chase is a different one. "I don't know that I'm your mate. We can't complete the mating until I'm sure."

He grabs my cheeks in his hands. "If you think you going alone, you're wrong. You're stuck with me. I don't fucking care who you're chasing, but I think it's part of your job. I will mark you, but not on the neck. I'm the alpha in my pack, it wouldn't look good if you're not marked. For now, we'll be quick, but you'll come with me after, and I'll make love to you the way it should be."

"I don't know you. What's your name?" I try to say.

His bright eyes are on me. "I'm Duncan, and I'm the alpha of the Grif Pack. What's your name?"

"I'm Cass....Casey." I don't know why, but I'm unable to lie to him about my name.

"You're Jade's best friend. I've heard about you." With that, his hand goes under my skirt and finds my center. I feel like I have a fever. He starts to kiss me and then licks and kisses my neck. My fangs emerge, and I want to drink from him. I want to taste his delicious blood, to mark him also.

"It's not possible."

"It is. You know about Jade, her mate is my beta and second-in-command. Now it's time for me to stake my claim. After you can find the person you're looking for, then we'll go to the hotel and mate properly."

With that, his finger starts to stroke my clit, and I buck against his hand. My brain is fogging, the sensations are too much. He kisses me and starts to play with my tits, but his mouth heads lower. He tosses my panties aside and begins to lick me. I scream. It's too much. I'm so close, he kisses the side of my thigh and licks it. He increases the movements of his finger to make me come.

"You're mine, come now."

Nobody has ever had power like he has over me. I've never let anyone—living or dead—have that kind of control. He bites me, and I come like I never have before. I see stars as I come against his finger. "Beautiful. Now mark me."

My brain takes control a little, and I need his taste, it's like a drug for me. Then I'm on my knees unzipping his pants. His dick is free, and I start to lick, and I can tell he loves it. I continue to stroke him as I stand and start to lick his neck at the same spot he licked me. I'm drooling now, I want a taste.

I bite him, and he screams and comes against my hand. He has his shirt up, and all his semen lands on his belly. His blood is like a drug, I almost come again from his taste, I can feel the connection. It seems that we share that trait with vampires during bonding with our need to taste our mate's blood. I remove my fangs and lick the wound.

"Fuck, I saw stars. I need to clean up and go with you on your mission. After, you're all mine. Do you feel the bond between us?"

I nod. My fangs are still out, and I'm breathless. He takes a few tissues and cleans himself before zipping his pants and putting his shirt where it belongs. "You've got some pretty small guns. You think you need those?"

I smile. "Maybe. Usually, I have my katana. Jade said it wasn't appropriate to bring it into the club."

He kisses me. "Come, let's find him, and then we can have the rest of the night for ourselves."

He takes my hand, and we leave the room and head back to the dance floor.

12. THE LADY

"MY LADY, WE'VE BEEN INFORMED that Casey is closing in on Damaris. They're in the club."

"That bitch," I scream, throwing my book against the wall. "She's got guts, I'll give her that. Which club?"

My personal assistant looks at the report. "They are at Jeremy's club, The Black Lotus. From what we understand, Damaris is trying to convert him to our cause."

I rub my temple. "Maybe that's a good idea, but I'm not sure anymore. We need to take care of him. We'll find another vampire to do our dirty work. Do you know if Jeremy can replace him?"

She smiles at me. "Well, my Lady, I know he can, because Donovan has already talked to him."

This is the end of Damaris then. He was always the weakest member of our team. A lot of people don't like him as He could bring us down. We need to get rid of him before Casey finds him.

She looks at me for instruction. "What is the plan, my Lady?"

"Easy, call Donovan and his mate, tell them to go there and bring Damaris to me right away. We need him here. I will personally take care of him when he's inside our walls. That way, he'll no longer be a threat to our plan."

She takes out her mobile and starts to text.

"I need him alive, but he needs to be controlled. Donovan has to secure Jeremy's position inside our organization. After that, we don't need Damaris."

A few seconds later, her phone buzzes with a reply. "Everything is set. Donovan will take care of it himself. I feel that he was waiting for this. Like he knew."

I smile. "He knows most of what's going on, but not all of it. What he does know is more than everyone else that joins our cause. They will know when the time has come." It's true that nobody knows all my reasons for wanting this unification, but I keep quiet. If everything goes the way I want it to, I'll be leader over all of them. It's brilliant. None of them know what's about to hit them, but for now, we need more magical artifacts. We need more supporters for our cause. I don't care who. I need soldiers to be on the front line and bring me what I need.

"We will succeed, my Lady, I guarantee it."

Of all my followers, I will miss her the most, but in the future, for the good of the mission, she needs to go, and I'll need another right-hand person. She's starting to discover too much. Not now as I still need her, but soon. She needs to go for me to be able to carry out the most significant part of my mission—my revenge.

13. CASEY

"STAY CLOSE TO ME. You're not alone anymore."

I roll my eyes. "I'm a fucking daywalker, I can defend myself. Don't think just because I don't have my katana on my body, I can't. It's in the car across the street. I'm not some weak woman that hides behind her mate."

He glares at me. "I knew you were going to be a pain. Stay alive, I need you. We both need you." With that, he kisses me. One thing's for sure, tonight isn't going like it was supposed to.

"Follow me and stay out of my way. I don't want to deal with this mission and with you trying to protect me."

Reaching the central part of the club, we head over to Jade and her mate. From the way she's smiling at me, she knows.

"Well, that's interesting."

I sigh. "Don't start. I need to find Damaris and bring him to Kane. I need him alive. We suspect he's not working alone and we need to know who he's working with."

Jade nods, but it's difficult to take her seriously with the broad grin on her face.

"What?"

Duncan is right behind me with his hand on my waist. It's a clear message that tells everyone in the room to back off, that I belong to him.

"We need to talk later. I need to teach you how to be a mate not just to a werewolf but to an alpha."

I turn to look around the room, searching. I need to find the goons to find Damaris.

"So, can you describe him?" Duncan asks.

"He's a vampire, and he has two human goons with him. You can't help me with this."

"And?"

"And nothing. That's all I'm telling you. You have to wait here."

He kisses me. "Not happening, sweetheart. Don't worry, from what I know, not a lot of vampires are here today so it's not going to be hard to figure out which one he is. Do you know if he knows someone is there looking for him?"

"Good question. I haven't had time to check. I need to see if Greg has found anything."

Duncan's eyes change color, turning bright yellow.

"What?" I ask him infuriated.

"I don't like that another male is helping you. Who he is?"

"Stop that. Before tonight I didn't know you. I know and trust him. Greg is part of the SIA Investigation Team. He's an excellent hacker. He can find anything anywhere. I haven't had time to contact him since someone kept me busy when I should have been checking in with him." My patience is thin. I hate this type of situation. There's a good reason I don't do relationships.

"I don't like it."

I slap his chest. "Tough. Stop being a moron, and maybe we can work together." I grab his arm just as he opens his mouth to speak. "There's one of the goons."

I'm pretty sure about it. I recognize his tattoo. I start to move, needing to follow him. There's no sign of Damaris, but I know he's here. It's easier to hunt someone when you're alone, but when you have a group of people following you, it gets complicated. I try to not be stubborn and throw a tantrum, but I need to focus on him, even with my mate growling at me. "Shut up!"

"I can't control him, we're not fully mated, and he wants to have the full bonding before you follow another male."

Please, give me patience. I really need it right now.

The goons head toward the kitchen, and I hear him speaking to someone. "Master, we have what you need."

I make a sign to silence the group before I head in that direction. I listen carefully. They aren't in the kitchen, but somewhere close to it.

"Good, you did well. Your master is very pleased."

"Damaris." Another male voice calls, a werewolf this time. I take a quick look.

"Yes, Donovan?"

Who's Donovan? He's a new player in the game.

"The Lady wants to see you now. You have the object?"

I see Damaris smile at his friend. "Yes, the Philosophers' Stone belongs to us. That warrior witch bitch couldn't stop us."

My hand is twitching now. I know that Jade can fight, but I'm the best at hand-to-hand combat. I miss my katana, but my guns will stay hidden just in case I need them.

Duncan starts to breathe behind my neck. "What's the plan?" he whispers in my ear.

I turn my head a little to look at him. "I need Damaris alive and not too damaged."

He laughs softly. "I'll do my best."

I grab him. "I'm serious. You want me to trust you, then do what I ask."

He shows me his teeth. "I'm the alpha here."

I sigh. "You really want to debate this now? My mission, my way, or you wait behind. You choose."

He nods, but I'm sure I will pay for it later.

When Donovan tells Damaris that the Lady, whoever she is, wants to see him, his face changed. If I didn't know better, I'd think he was besotted. That's interesting, but who she is? That's one of the questions Damaris will need to answer.

Jade moves with her mate to the other side of the door. We have no choice but to enter and start a fight. It's the only outcome.

I kiss my mate. "Don't get killed."

He smiles, and I open the door wide.

"Damaris, I'm here for you," I yell at him.

"Fuck that, fucking daywalker."

The goon pulls out his gun, but my mate jumps on him and starts to beat him. My focus is on Damaris, he is my target.

"You bring that fucking daywalker here, Damaris?"

I start to run, and Damaris takes out his guns. It's funny, but that's the last thing I would've thought he'd bring with him. The human is easy to immobilize, and my mate heads toward Donovan. I can feel Jade right behind me.

"You're a pain in my ass, Casey, and not the good kind."

I smile evilly. "I'm happy to see you've been thinking of me. If you weren't, I'd be sad and pout." My fangs and claws are ready, and Damaris is ready too. I need to remove that fucking gun he has.

"You'll never catch me. The Lady will bring reinforcements to save me. I'm her favorite."

"You're delusional, Damaris. You're a fucking vampire that fucked up, and now you're going to pay. Oh, and Kane said to tell you he has a surprise waiting just for you."

"His fucking bitch should have been killed. I'll make sure next time I don't miss."

I attack and force him to drop the guns. "You've got no chance against me, Damaris. You may be older, but I'm stronger." I slam my head against him, which makes him shake a little and back up.

"You'll pay for that, bitch." He charges me, and with no gun, it's strength against strength.

"I have a strong head. Did you see stars?" I'm having fun now, I love it when they resist.

"Here, Master, right here." I recognize his other goon's voice.

I take one of my guns from under my skirt and shoot him. A direct hit to his shoulder. "You have nowhere to hide, Damaris. You can run but I will find you."

The human shoots at me, but from the bullet he chose, he doesn't know much about us daywalkers.

I hear a growl from Duncan. He can chase me if he wants, but I have my own prey to catch, and he's close. Damaris heads toward the back door trying to escape.

I see both werewolves—my mate and Donovan—head toward the door. They're fighting and I sense Donovan is also an alpha. Usually, the fight between alphas is for dominance, but if one has a mate in danger, it means there's more reason to fight.

"Jade, the car door."

I start to run toward the car, I need my katana. She unlocks the door remotely, and I open it. *There it is.* I grab it and start to run. Damaris is in front of me, and I have Donovan chasing me also.

My main focus is Damaris, that son of a bitch has got to go. He turns and heads down a small ally where the light is poor.

He stops at the end and turns to look at me. He removes his coat and takes something out from his back. "Casey, you're not the only one that has a katana. I'm a master of it."

I smile. People can tell me I'm crazy, but I love fighting like this. "Bring it on, old man!"

He charges and I'm able to block it easily. I hear another fight start behind me and I know my mate is still fighting Donovan.

"Is he your mate, dear Casey? I hope you've completed your mating. I'm guessing my friend will kill him. You know the only outcome between two alphas is the death of one of them."

I start to worry a little at Damaris's words. I've never worried about my life. I need to trust Duncan and his ability to look after himself and fight. I'll never mate with a weak man. "We'll see. I have faith in him. He can take care of himself." With that, I hear him howling at the moon. I don't need an interpreter to know he's happy with my reply to this piece of shit.

I charge Damaris again, our blades clash against one another. He is strong, but at the same time, he's weak. I need to bring him in alive. I feel the sun is getting close to rising. It may not affect me the same way as it does full vampires, but I still have the calling each morning—I'm part vampire after all. Damaris's eyes are red. I suspect mine are as well. Our fangs are out. I decide to claw him and blood starts to flow, but he has hidden a small blade. He pulls it out and slashes me with it. I scream, but I'm pissed off more than hurt. I don't mind the small scratch, but I need to put him down.

"That hurt, little Casey? I have plenty more where that came from."

I hear my mate growling and direct my words to him. "Don't mind me, it's not my first scratch and won't be the last. Keep him busy. I need Damaris out of commission for transportation."

Damaris tries to slash me again, but this time I dodge and do a spinning back kick that hits him in his face.

"No!" a woman screams.

I hit my target with both blades before jumping on him and punching him.

Jade arrives beside me and takes his sword. "Don't kill him."

I raise my head enough to see that a witch has started to cast a spell on my mate because he's winning against Donovan. I punch Damaris's face as hard as I can and put him out of commission.

Jade and her mate take control of Damaris, and I run as fast as I can toward my mate. He's won the fight. Donovan had no chance against him.

"You're going to release him." I grab my mate and pull him away just as a spell hits beside us. "You've got some guts, witch. That's my mate, and I don't like that you're trying to kill him."

She moves next to Donovan. "Don't piss me off, daywalker. Never mess with a fire witch. He almost killed my mate."

I know physically I'm superior to her as only a warrior witch can equal me in a fight. I can tell her power is great though as her fireball was powerful, but my katana blade has an enchantment on it that neutralizes any spells against it.

I start to walk toward her, and my mate tries to stop me. "Have faith in me like I did with you." He releases me. My blade is ready, my training is there. I need to protect my mate.

I can see Donovan trying to stop her, which makes her hesitate for a second before she releases her spell. My katana stops it, and I charge toward them, but when the smoke fades, they have disappeared. She's teleported them some-where. I look at Jade and her mate. They have Damaris on the ground, still out of commission. I turn and see my mate on his feet, and he pulls me against him. Who is this fucking *Lady* Damaris spoke of? Was it that witch?

14. THE LADY

HIDDEN BASE SOMEWHERE IN THE MONTREAL NEUTRAL zone

"ARGGG!"

I can hear the sound of something breaking, then my assistant comes into the room, followed by Donovan and his mate. "My Lady, we lost Damaris. Casey has managed to capture him. We almost lost Donovan and his mate as well."

"And the object?" I don't like it. I never lose to anyone. That bitch Casey is on my permanent list of mortal enemies. Not only does she have Damaris, who can spill a lot of secrets, but they might also have the one thing that could give me invisibility.

"Lost, my Lady."

I want to hit something, it's so wrong.

"My Lady, we failed." Donovan enters the room with his mate who is trying to heal him. He's in terrible shape, but I'm sure he will recover.

His mate speaks. "Casey had help. I think she has a mate. Her friend from Internal Affairs helped as well."

"Daywalkers never mate."

"We never thought a werewolf and a witch would mate either but it's happened. We don't know how fate will present them to us. She has his mark. It's not visible, but another shifter will know she's off the market, and so is her friend Jade."

"She's a daywalker as well?"

"Yes, my Lady."

"She wasn't on the list of agents at Internal Affairs Grant provided me. She's supposed to be working for him and not against us." That complicates things too.

"Finding your mate can change things. I suspect she's been spying for Casey."

I try to think and fast. The Investigation Team knows something is going on and that vampires, werewolves, and witches are working together. The object they have is useful but doesn't tell them more than that. "Donovan, you fought well today, go heal with your mate. I'm sure Casey will be back one way or another. Now isn't the time for more. Damaris will stay loyal to us, and we will rescue him soon."

"Very well, my Lady. If you need us, let us know."

I nod at him, and they leave.

"My Lady, what do we do next?" my assistant asks.

I look at her. "Nothing for now. I'm sure the Investigation Team won't kill him. He only knows minimal information about us, but we do need to get those magical objects faster."

"We have increased our new followers already. Jeremy has agreed to join us although he's asking what happened to Damaris."

That is excellent news. "Tell him the truth, tell him that Casey took him to the Investigation Team for questioning and they are keeping him prisoner. No more than that. He's joined us willingly?"

"Yes, he has. Damaris explained everything to him."

I'm pleased as it means even though we've lost Damaris, we are still in a position to corrupt more vampires with Jeremy's help.

"Tell him what he needs to know. We'll start him the same way we did Damaris. Tell him we're going to try to rescue Damaris, but his gifts are needed somewhere else. Give him the same bullshit we gave Damaris, and we'll adjust after."

"Very well, my Lady, I will inform him. Do we send a rescue team?"

I grin at her. "No, don't bother. He doesn't need to know the truth just yet."

She nods and leaves me.

What a night. What should have been a simple thing, to retrieve a magical object, ended up where I almost lost one of my best soldiers. Luckily, his mate protects him. I knew from the beginning that Damaris was trouble. Now I don't care if he rots. I will concentrate my efforts on Jeremy. He will bring more vampires to our cause. I will get my revenge on those who banned me—not only them but their followers as well. They will perish.

15. CASEY

WHAT A NIGHT. DAMARIS HAS BEEN CAUGHT, AND I'M at the infirmary at the Investigation Team headquarters with my mate, Jade, and Dean. That's what they call a hundred and eighty -degree turn. I look at my mate. I know nothing about him, but at the same time, it's like I've known him all my life. One of the healer witches has cast a spell to help him heal from his wounds after his fight with Donovan.

"You're good, it's nothing you can't heal from." She smiles at him and nods at me.

Kane enters the infirmary and starts to tease me. "So, you decided to have a party without me?"

"Sorry, Kane, I only had one invitation, but at the same time, I discovered a mate." Just then, my mate stands and puts one arm around my neck. "I'm Duncan"

"Kane." The two men shake hands as Kane smiles at us both. "I see that. I've always been told daywalkers couldn't mate. Now I discover there's not one but two that are mated."

"Believe me, I have no idea how it happened, but I suspect there's more than the two of us. And speaking of mates, the werewolf that was there—Donovan— seems to be mated to a witch." I look at my mate, and he kisses me.

"Witch, you say?"

"Yes, a fire witch to be precise, a powerful one too."

Kane takes a deep breath before letting it out slowly. "That's not good."

I look at him while my mate starts to stroke my hair. I'm not used to this, but at the same time, I love it. "Why?"

"Not here. We need a debriefing. I'm guessing you're not going back to Internal Affairs?"

I look at my mate, we haven't talked about anything yet, we need time for ourselves.

Duncan speaks before I can. "Casey and I haven't had time to talk about it yet. If it was up to me, I'm pretty sure we'd be at a hotel and mating until we can't walk, but her mission was important. I don't have all the details, but from what I've seen, you've got a lot of problems and not just within the vampire faction. I'm guessing werewolves, shifters, and witches, and who knows who else are involved. I'm the Grif Pack's alpha, and we will help however we can. Not only my mate but my beta's mate are involved in this. No one tries to kill one of ours."

I see Jade and Dean coming closer and Duncan quickly introduces them to Kane.

"We'll have that meeting now. Lizbeth will not be there since it's daylight, but I'll tell her everything when she wakes."

The four of us follow Kane inside a big conference room where several others are already waiting. "Everyone, please take a seat, we have news we need to share with you all. First of all, Damaris is in our custody, and he also had a magical object. Let me introduce Casey and Jade who are daywalkers and their mates, Duncan and Dean who are part of the Grif Pack. This is Ross, Kass, one of the Elders—but just call him

Elder—Gwen, Tessa, and Debra. They're part of this investigation and are also Internal Affairs within the witch faction. Tell us everything you know, Casey."

"It's a pleasure to meet you all. I wish it were under different circumstances, but here's what we know so far." I start with my first meeting with Kane and Lizbeth and my research into what's going on.

"You think that your boss is working with them?" Gwen, one of the witches, asks.

"He's been acting weird for a couple of weeks. He's never involved himself in our missions before. That's not his job, and he knows it. He's a vampire, but his maker was killed a century ago, so he's similar to a daywalker. Usually, blood ties prevail in the vampire faction, but now we know from Damaris's actions there are things that can make them betray those blood ties. If that's true, it confirms what we've suspected. Before today, almost everyone thought a daywalker couldn't mate, that we are only there to serve as a kind of police force inside the vampire faction. Now it's different." I continue with my intervention at Jeremy's club.

"Could Jeremy help us, or do you think Damaris has corrupted him?" Kane asks me.

"I'm not sure. I didn't see him. I'm guessing he's provided blood and probably sex to Damaris, but I haven't had time to investigate that part yet."

Silence surrounds us as every person in the room thinks hard about what's going on. "What is your conclusion so far?" the Elder asks.

"I'm not sure, I know something is going on. What that is, I can't say. I'm not saying it's not normal for members of different factions to help each other, it's just odd. We coexist, but at the same time, we don't. The neutral zone is the place that each species can interact with another, but they aren't allowed to be on faction ground if they're not part of that faction. Maybe it's others like us that have mated with other species inside the community and are frustrated with the way things are and are behind it. The blood link is strong, but the mating bond is stronger."

Everyone starts to talk at the same time.

"Silence!" Kane yells to all of us. "Don't start jumping to conclusions. We have a situation on our hands that needs more than just the Investigation Team to figure out. Each of your factions will have to help. I have a feeling it's only the tip of the iceberg. More will come, and we'll need to be ready. For the first time since the beginning of time, we need to work with each other. We'll be the central hub of information, and you're welcome to come and share and learn what others know in all this." Kane tells everyone.

"What about the object?" I ask.

"That's easy, a warrior witch will be here soon. We know the stone has to be retrieved by one of them and taken to the Librarian for safety. The stone needs its witch to retrieve it," Debra explains.

"The Librarian has already been in contact. There's no need for them both to be here at the same time," Kane tries to reassure her.

"You don't understand. If a warrior witch doesn't find her piece, and it's not lost to an evil hand, her magic is affected. In that case, one of the witches will be in pain because of this. She needs to give it to the Librarian for her own sake."

Interesting. I haven't educated myself on the other factions since my role was simple. It was to bring any vampire within the faction back into line with our laws.

"Very well, we will wait for the witch to come here," Kane tells her. "Do we have anything else to discuss? Anyone have any more information?"

The Elder speaks. "We have another problem, but we don't think it's part of what's happening here."

"Meaning?" Kane asks.

"Gorad, the black wizard, has started to free himself. We've tried to prevent it and the Special Operations Team is working with us on it, but as I said, I don't think they're related. We're trying to figure out what happened. I will tell you that inter-species mating is growing and we will see it more and more. Throughout history, we've had some inter-species pairs, but I think it will become the norm in a couple of years."

"If you're right, that'll become a problem with faction borders."

"Maybe we need to rethink those borders. Humans that mingle between species are starting to be common, but now we have witches mated to werewolves and vampires, a vampire that's mated half-demon, and a daywalker mated to a werewolf. What other pairings will we have? Breeding between the factions could cause problems," the Elder explains.

"The only one that doesn't need to breed is a vampire. They create new ones," Kane says.

The Elder shakes his head. "No, it doesn't work like that. Those that are turned are considered weak inside the vampire faction. They can never have a baby with another vampire. Witches or other species could be possible, but we're not sure. But a turned vampire is sterile with another vampire. Even for them, they are starting to have problems producing children. The only species that can have a baby with them, except another vampire, is a full human that hasn't been turned, but that seems to only happen if they are fated mates."

I think about this information. We've been blind for so many centuries.

"That means what exactly?" my mate asks the Elder.

"It means that nature always looks for balance. We

created an unbalance for centuries with the factions. Lucky for all of us, the neutral zone brings a sort of balance, but I think that nature wants more from us. Tell me, Duncan, have you noticed that inbreeding has become a problem within your faction?"

"Yes, I have. A lot of us are going to the neutral zone, hoping to find a mate. Dean and I have been lucky to find ours, but it also means we can no longer live within the faction, only the neutral zone," Duncan replies.

The Elder shakes his head. "There it is. Not only do we have some that are starting to rebel because of those rules, but we see inter-species mating that didn't exist twenty years ago. The situation is bigger than that. We're facing a rebellion but also a revolution. People are desperate to find their fated one. So much so that they're looking at other clans and factions."

It really is bigger than we thought.

"Will each faction or clan provide support?" Kane asks us.

"As for Jade and me, I can confirm we will work with you. I don't know about the rest of the group, but I can try to communicate with the rogue ones that have disappeared all of a sudden," I reply.

"As for my pack, you have our support. As I said, not only my mate but my beta's mate are part of this, which means we're now involved. I don't know about the rest of the packs within the shifter faction, but I can ask around and see what happens," Duncan answers.

"The witches' Internal Affairs, are with you. I don't know if each coven will do it, but I can tell you we'll do our part. We'll inform our community about this and see what they say, but if we tell them that other factions are joining with you, it brings more emphasis and maybe people will talk," Gwen replies.

"We, the Elders, will help the best we can, but we also

have to help the Special Operations Team at the Paranormal University solve the other problem. We'll advise you if anything changes with Gorad."

Kane nods at us. "Great, we'll keep each other posted through the secure channel we've set up. If it's something big, we'll meet. As for us, the Investigation Team is in one hundred percent and more so in my case, since my mate is also involved. Damaris is out of commission, but that doesn't mean others won't want her dead."

I nod and pull Kane aside as everyone leaves. "Kane, I want to see Damaris. I need to interrogate him."

He smiles at me. "I was sure you'd say that. I already have him in a room. Come. Let's get it done, and you can be with your mate later. We have a room here. It will be more private for you guys." With that, Kane hands me a keycard in a paper folder, similar to what they give out in hotels—a quick glance shows it's a room on the fourth floor—and shows us the way to where they're holding Damaris.

16. DAMARIS

I'M CHAINED TO A chair and I've lost some blood, but I'll survive. That bitch has me, but I know they'll come to rescue me. My mission has failed again. Not only have I not taken care of Lizbeth, but now one of my top priorities is to make Casey pay for what she's done.

I hope Jeremy joins our cause as we need another vampire. I've spread the news of what's happening, but I haven't had time to talk to anyone else. I know vampires love to gossip, and if someone is talking at the underground level, it's good. If Jeremy also joins us, it's even better. He's the first one I've contacted directly.

When I woke it was dark and I don't know how long I was unconscious. Why did Donovan come to me? We were supposed to meet after I'd convinced Jeremy to join us. The light and the lack of decor starts to piss me off. How long will they keep me like this? The door opens, and someone from the Investigation Team enters.

"I see you're awake," the woman says to me.

"Yes, and you are?"

"My name isn't important. It's more the message I bring."

I look at her, wondering who the fuck she is. "Fine, what's the message?"

"Don't worry, I have clearance to be here, but the Lady doesn't want you released just yet."

My body freezes at her name. "What?"

She smiles at me. "You don't know me, and I'm not part of the SIA. What you see now is a vision. It's in your head. I have your blood with me, so I'm able to connect to you through your mind. That's my power. As I said, she will not rescue you. Well, not right now at least."

Am I dreaming? A vampire doesn't dream. I didn't know anyone could do something like this. We have some people that have mutated and evolved but nothing like this. "Tell me why?"

"Simple, she needs you here for now."

I'm angry at this decision. "I don't know why you're here. Are you going to kill me?" If she is, I'd prefer to know now.

"Tsk! Tsk! You're not in a position to ask or request. The Lady is very disappointed with you. You were the only vampire we were able to corrupt so fast. We knew you hated your brother and his son, so we took advantage."

I try to free myself. I need her out of my mind.

"Don't try, it won't work. This isn't real, it's only a dream."

"Vampires don't fucking dream."

She laughs. "Well, there's a lot more going on than you know. The old species aren't the only ones that have abilities and want change. There are a lot of hybrids that do as well."

"Hybrids?"

"You think half-demons are the only half-breeds? We've been inter-species mating for decades now, and the result is stunning. You know enough for now. If you don't say anything about us, we may rescue you. You need to be a good boy. If not, we'll make sure you don't survive."

I open my eyes, and she isn't there anymore. *Am I still*

dreaming? What did she mean by hybrids? That's not the original plan, but I've always wondered if I knew it all. I need to try and contact Jeremy, I need to get free. I'm stuck here, these chains prove that. Have I made a mistake? If I have, I've no choice but to follow her instructions. I'm in too deep, and I need to live. I'm not ready to become dust.

What are my options? Stay silent, and hope they rescue me or tell them what I know —which obviously isn't as much as I thought it was. I need to decide on a strategy fast. I'm not in the right place. If I stay here and say nothing, I'm sure Kane will want his revenge, but if I say what I do know, one, they probably won't believe me and two, my life will be on a timer, and I won't know when my time is up.

I need to decide and fast. I'm guessing Casey or Kane will join me soon, possibly both of them. By now, they know I'm awake.

I take a deep breath which doesn't do much since a vampire doesn't breathe, but it always allows me to re-center myself.

The door opens, and Casey enters with the werewolf that was fighting with Donovan, maybe I was right when I was taunting her, she has got a mate. It's showtime, and I need to act like I'm supposed to.

17. CASEY

"I HOPE YOU GOT A GOOD NIGHT'S SLEEP, Damaris. Now, I need answers, and don't fuck with me."

Duncan chuckles at my back, and I grin at his reaction.

"I've got nothing to say to you, bitch!"

Before I have time to react, my mate has his hand around Damaris's neck. "You'd better be nice if not, I'll take it personally. No one messes with my mate."

Part of me is thrilled with Duncan's possessiveness. Nobody has ever stood up for me like that, I've been alone for so long. "Calm down. Damaris will be the perfect vampire gentleman. Right, Damaris?"

My mate releases him but hits him as he does. I know that losing blood is not good for a vampire, and we need him to survive, but that doesn't mean we can't hurt him a little.

"You've really mated with that dog?" I need to know for sure.

I look at my mate. He smiles at me tenderly, but when his eyes go back to Damaris, I can see he's fighting his wolf. It's in his bright yellow eyes. "I did, so you see, Damaris, we know something is happening in our community, but it's not totally clear what the intention is. You'll provide me information. I asked Kane if I could talk to you first and you know what'll happen if I get nothing. You'll be at the mercy of the half-demon. And not even being a vampire will protect you from his fury."

Damaris spits blood on the table. "I don't know much. You've stopped me from meeting the head of the organization, so my knowledge is limited."

Fuck, well we'll have to make do with what he can tell us. "First things first. You were with Donovan. He was really keen to have you back. What's your relationship with him and his pack?"

"Not much, he's my contact. Which I'm sure you've already guessed," Damaris tells me, without revealing anything new.

"That witch was his mate. Is she the head of the organization?" I ask directly.

"No, she's only his mate."

His words confirm that witches are also participating in inter-species mating.

"Who's the person in charge?"

He looks at me and grins. "I don't know who it is. I don't even know their name. You caught the wrong person for that."

I hit the table. "Don't fuck with me, Damaris. I know you know more about this organization. What are their plans? What did they promise you?"

He stays silent.

"You know Kane comes after me. He doesn't care what information you have. He just wants you to hurt."

Damaris's eyes change. "I don't know anything."

I grab his shirt, and my fangs are out. "Internal Affairs doesn't control me anymore." His eyes widen at my statement. "Yes, now you're starting to understand. I can do anything I want to you, and no one will stop me."

He licks his lips. "I don't care, Casey. You may not be part of Internal Affairs anymore, but the Investigation Team won't let you do what you want. They have rules and regulations. You have some latitude but not much, and if I decide to keep my mouth shut, you can't make me talk."

I punch him in his face. His head wobbles back and forth. "Maybe not, but that doesn't mean I can't enjoy part of this interrogation. You know I can make you talk. I have my ways, and they are legal, just so you know."

I head toward my mate and start kissing him, and he follows my lead. One thing a vampire doesn't like, if they are in need of blood, is to see others get it and have fun doing so.

"You're a kinky girl," Duncan says, smiling.

I kiss him quickly. "You have a lot to learn about me, and one of the things is that I'm not good at relationships."

"Being a mate is different, you know that."

I head back toward Damaris.

"You've mated with a dog, you can't get lower than that."

I see red and start to punch him repeatedly. "Watch your mouth or I may hurt you more than that. Talk and fast." I'm pissed off, the fucker will pay.

He spits blood on the floor. "I've had worse. I'll tell you everything. He'll know if I'm lying." Damaris points his chin to my mate.

"You're right, bloodsucker," Duncan says and then looks at me. "So, far, he's telling the truth."

"That may be true, but the small details he has can lead to something. That's what I need. Kane will have his fun after I'm finished. I don't think he'll be in any shape after that to talk to me. I need him to talk now." I smile at Damaris. "We'll start again. Why were you at Jeremy's club?"

"Simple, I needed blood and sex."

"Why that club and not another one? I'm sure that's not the only one that could help you. You could have gone to Alto's club." I'm testing him to see his reaction, and it's just what I was hoping for as he screams at me.

"That bitch took everything from me, and she'll pay for that."

I know Kane is behind the glass. He's monitoring everything I do in case he hears something I don't in all the excitement.

"Damaris, a bit of advice friend, stop calling Lizbeth a bitch because I know Kane is taking note of each time you call her that, and it will make your beating worse."

He looks at the one-way glass. "He can kill me, I don't care. I'm not going to talk, and within this organization, he can't do what he wants," Damaris says, and starts to laugh. "All of you are already screwed, and you don't even know it. You better brace yourself for what's coming soon."

Damaris is in bad shape, but his anger is stronger than the rest.

"What did they promise you that made you betray your blood?"

"Nothing that concerns you." He's playing the fierce vampire right now.

I chuckle. "You know, Damaris, if you don't talk to me, Kane will have his way. We know that you know stuff, and we wonder what their promise was to you. I think it's something big and you've corrupted Jeremy in the process."

He stays silent, and I know I've hit the mark with that. I look at my mate. He smiles at me, it's like a game for him.

"Fine, you don't want to talk. Kane will take the next round, and you know what'll happen?" Damaris shakes his head. "Well, if you don't have anything to say to me, and Kane can't get you to talk either, Alto will be pleased to have you back. You've brought shame to his blood, and the sentence for that is not only death by sun but torture as well. You know he's done that in the past."

He flinches a little. "How do you know he isn't part of this?"

"Because if that was the case, you wouldn't be here and being hunted not only by us but by him as well. Alto can be a son of a bitch, but lying is not in his dictionary. He's put good money on your head, and since I have no place to go now I'm mated, and I have to stay in the neutral zone, it's a tempting offer."

"This organization will not let you do that. Their regulations—"

"Fuck their regulations. They don't want you if you don't know anything. They'll have no use for you. The only reason you're here is because of me and my mission and the fact you almost killed Lizbeth. But after Kane and I have our fun, you're no use to them, and we know Alto will kill you. For us, that's good enough." I turn my back on him and take my mate's hand before turning my head back to him. "We'll give you time to think it over. If you decide not to cooperate, it's the last time you'll see me. Just know I'll be alive and well while you're suffering and dying. You better start talking if you want to live. If not, after Kane has his fun, I will contact Alto and arrange a meeting with him." I don't wait for his answer, and we leave.

Duncan grabs me around the waist as soon as the door closes behind us. "You think that was a good idea?"

"He knows what his brother can do. I've witnessed in the past what kind of horror he's capable of. He's not just upset at him, he's angry. Alto's reputation is on the line. He's old-fashioned, and if we send him back, he'll torture Damaris, and it won't be in private. It'll be done in public for his clan see and to remind them the price of betraying his blood. For vampires, blood is sacred. It would be like if your mate cheated on you. You think it's impossible, but if it happens, you know what you'd do."

He nods at me, understanding in his eyes.

Kane joins us. "So, he didn't talk?"

"No. I'm sure he knows something, but not a lot. We need to know why he betrayed his blood. That could help us in this investigation and help catch everyone working with them."

Kane looks at the door.

"He knows you can't kill him, but you can hurt him badly. After you finish, if he hasn't told you anything, we'll give it twenty-four hours to think and come up with a plan. Our best bet will be Alto's reputation and maybe playing on that without letting him know we have Damaris. We'll have limited time, since gossip in the community is rolling, and maybe some of his blood family will report that we have him," I tell Kane.

"Maybe, but until then we can play with him a bit and try to find out more information. He's hiding something. He didn't lie, but he didn't tell the whole truth either," Kane says and heads toward the door and Damaris.

"So, what do we do now?" Duncan asks.

I put my arm around his neck. "Well, we have a room here, and I know it's soundproof."

Once again he throws me over his shoulder like a sack of potatoes and heads to the elevator as I laugh at him. "Which floor?"

I hit the fourth floor, and when the doors open, I give him directions to the room. Handing him the key card that Kane gave me earlier, I can almost pretend we are in a hotel and not Investigation Agency guest quarters.

18. THE LADY

"MY LADY?"

My assistant brings me back to reality as she enters the room. "What is it?"

She approaches me with a piece of paper in her hand. "From what our contact has said, they're going to contact Alto to retrieve Damaris from the Investigation Team."

I look through the window of the building. "When?"

I hear paper shuffling. "Midnight, two days from now."

"That could complicate things. Do you know if Jeremy knows?"

She looks to the floor. "He's the one that brought us the news. I guess he's preparing to rescue him. Apparently, Jeremy has someone on in the inside that's able to provide him information. He doesn't know everything, but the few things he's been told is quality information."

I can feel my headache returning. "That's not good. They

already know too much for my liking, and if that happens, it'll be bad for us. We will need to move up the timetable even more if we want to reverse the factions and be a neutral zone."

"Yes, my Lady, it's not good, but we knew it could happen."

"You're right, but not right now. We're not strong enough. We need more magical objects to help us. The fact Damaris was captured means more digging from the Investigation Team into us. So far, they don't know who the head of our group is, and I intend to keep it that way." I don't need them to know anything that could lead them to us. "Where's Donovan?"

"He's still healing. His mate is helping him, and he's still not in any condition to go on a mission." My little assistant is firm in the way she says it.

"Meaning he's fucking his mate to heal himself. No one can stop Jeremy?"

She shakes her head.

"Damn it. We don't need this."

"We could move before he does and compromise his plan."

"And how will you do that?"

"I could go ahead of him and make some noise. That way they'll think someone is there, without him getting caught. At the same time, I can pretend to save Jeremy, which will make him loyal to our cause."

I play with my long hair. "That could work. You know what you have to do?"

She nods and leaves. It's a good plan. It's better if Jeremy doesn't rescue Damaris, but we need to make him see that. I need more objects, I need more magic. To conquer them all, I need them to make me more powerful, make them my slaves. I will mark the ones that harmed me and get my revenge. It will be perfect. I'll be in charge, and they'll have to bow to me. I'll have power over everyone's lives. It's perfect. Every one that was against me will suffer the consequence. I need this. That is my due, and they will become my slaves or die.

19. CASEY

DUNCAN GRINS AT ME. "Now, we have all the time we need, and I want to fuck and mark my mate. Do you have any objections?"

I smile at him and shake my head. The day will never come where I object to him fucking me. He starts to kiss me —hard and passionate. It's like he wants to possess me entirely and I'm happy to give in to him.

I rip his shirt needed to see him naked. I've dreamed about it since last night at the club.

"Impatient, mate?"

I chuckle. "Maybe but I'll let you see how impatient for yourself." I put my leg around his waist. I need to feel him, all of him.

"Not so fast. I'm the one in charge."

I chuckle. "Dream on, mate, I'm in charge here."

His hands are under my ass, and he carries me toward the bed before throwing me on it. I'm breathless like he is. "I'm the alpha."

"Maybe but that also makes me an alpha so don't mess

with me." I smile. I want to see him naked. I need to feel all his muscles and trace their pattern. "I need you naked."

"What're you willing to give me?"

I chew my lower lip. "I need you to fuck me and mark me the correct way. I want another taste of your blood. I'm drooling here, and that's not the only part of me that's wet."

He hisses at my statement. I want to submit to him but not make it easy. He needs to work for it.

"What does my mate want?"

"Strip!" I grab my phone and pull up the song 'Pony', so he has a beat.

"Very well, but I need the same from you. I need a private show from you as well."

I nod and wait for him. I start the song, and he starts to remove his shirt and moves those fucking abs. My eyes begin to bleed, and I want to touch my pussy.

"No playing, you're not naked, and I need my show. We'll play after."

He dances like a god, all his muscles move to the music. He removes his shoes and socks. The only thing that remains is his pants.

"I want them off. I need to see you completely naked."

He grins and starts to slowly unbuckle his belt, *that fucker*. I need to restrain myself. If I don't, I'll jump on him and have my way with him.

He starts to unbutton his pants and lowers the zipper. I see that he isn't wearing boxers or briefs—he's fucking naked under those pants. "It's faster when you need to transform." He must have been able to tell from my expression what I was thinking. His dick points at me. That's my invitation. I start crawling on all fours like a wolf and head toward my target. I want his dick in my mouth again.

His pants fall to the floor, and I lick my lips. I want to

taste him, and we have all the time we need. I crawl slower. His eyes turn bright yellow, and I can see he's beginning to lose control. I get closer to my prize, put my hand on his thigh, and pull myself to my knees. He doesn't say anything, but I look in his eyes and see pure lust there. I start to lick him slowly.

"Don't torture me. Put it in your mouth."

I comply—I want it anyway—and put the head of dick inside my mouth, and start to suck it. I've drooled over his dick since my first taste but I didn't have the time then to make him suffer a little.

"Ah, fuck, that mouth of yours. I knew it would be like this." All his muscles tense. "Shit, I need more." He backs away and looks at me. He's totally naked, and I'm still fully dressed. "It's your turn to strip now."

I gesture for him to get on the big king size bed which he does, and he starts to play with his dick.

I want him out of control, I'm too close to losing mine. I wink at him, and he puts the song on again. It's the best one to do a strip-tease to. I start to open my blouse slowly button by button.

"More," he orders with his deep, needy voice.

I remove my blouse, only to show my bra. I start to work on my skirt. Slowly, I turn around and show him the thong I'm wearing.

"Ah, fuck, that ass of yours."

I smile. I feel sexy and sensual. He gives that to me. I wonder if it is because I'm his mate.

"Tell me what you're thinking," he orders.

"I'm thinking how different you make me feel, and that I've never experienced anything like this. I wonder if it's because you're my mate."

I let go of the skirt, and it falls to the floor. I kick it away, along with my shoes, and slowly lift my leg to the bed and start to remove the nylon stockings and roll them down my leg.

"Casey, I need you right now."

I don't comply with his demand and do the same thing with the other leg until I'm standing in front of him, only wearing my bra and thong.

"Remove it."

I smile. I start with the bra and cup my breasts before I release it, and I hear a hiss from him. I turn around and begin to remove the thong and show him my ass and my pussy from behind. I hear him moving on the bed.

"I wanted to go slow, but that's impossible now." He grabs me and pushes me on my back on the bed.

"If you think that I'll submit—"

He grins. "I never thought you would. I love the fact you want my dick and the fact I'm the only one that makes you feel like this."

I moan. The fucker knows how to turn me on.

"We'll go slow the next time. Right now, I need to mark and possess you."

With that, he enters me swiftly, and I arch my back to take him more deeply inside me.

"Yes, you're so tight."

He starts to move, the friction between his dick and my pussy gives me goosebumps. I want it all, I need it all. He starts to play with my clit then.

"Duncan!" I scream his name when I come. I want to bite him, but he won't allow me to. "You don't want it?" I ask sadly at his refusal.

"I do want it, but if I let you, I'll come, and that's not what I want."

I feel his dick get bigger, he's close to coming. I'm still on cloud nine and don't register that he's moved me until I'm on all fours and he enters me again. He wants to claim his mate like a wolf.

20. DUNCAN

I NEED TO MARK HER, HER NECK IS NOT AN OPTION but the back of her neck—yes. With her long hair, nobody will see it. I start moving slowly, I want to build her want, I need her ready for what's coming. She's my mate, my wolf and I accept it. I take her hair and move it to the side before I put my arms around her waist and lift her, so her back is against my torso and starts to lick the back of her neck.

"I, Duncan, make my claim on you. You belong to me as I belong to you. It's for the rest of our lives. No other will take your place. We will become one." With that, I bite her hard. Her pussy grips my dick like her life depends on it. I almost see stars, but I need to contain myself.

"Yes, harder."

My mate wants more, and I will provide it. My balls hurt right now. All my body wants is release. I disengage from her, and she pushes me against the bedhead until I'm sitting.

"I, Casey, make my claim on you. You belong to me as I belong to you. For the rest of our lives. No other will take your place. We will become one."

She impales herself on me with her last words, and my

dick is back inside her. She grins at me. She pushes my head to the side and rides me hard. I won't be able to control myself for long. Her eyes are red, and her fangs are there to play. She starts to lick before biting me hard and starts to drink.

"Casey!" I scream as my seed releases and hits inside her. She's full of my cum, which will let other species know she belongs to me. I come hard. I've never come this hard before. I almost pass out from the pleasure. She licks my wound, and both of us are breathless. She moves off me, and my seed starts to drip down her leg a little. I put her on the bed, her back against my chest. I've never spooned before, but this is different. I start to kiss my mark on the back of her neck.

"And now?"

"We are mates. That means where you go, I go. My pack will accept you. You're strong, no other female will challenge your position."

She chuckles. "You know what I can do."

I smile against her skin. "I know. We need to get some sleep. We still have a lot to do, and now we need peace."

She strokes my arms. I notice that her breath is steady and I guess she's fallen asleep. I join her with a smile. Our life will not be perfect, but we will have each other, and that's all that matters. I never thought that by going to the club I'd find my mate, although I should have expected it as my beta mated another daywalker. Since they are friends, it will be easier for the pack to accept her. She starts to move her ass against my dick. He wants to play, and I'm hard again. She needs her sleep, but tomorrow morning, I will feast.

21. CASEY

TODAY WE ARE GIVING DAMARIS TO ALTO. HE chose not to talk, so we have no choice. It didn't help that Alto found out we had him thanks to the gossip. We have the guarantee Alto will never come against Lizbeth and he promises to kill Damaris after he's played with him.

Duncan enters our room. "Ah, there you are, love."

We've stayed with the Investigation Team until Damaris is handed back to Alto. I've learned that my boss has gone missing and more daywalkers have also gone rogue. Internal Affairs is almost empty. I don't know what will happen with this. The remaining ones want me to take over as head of the department, but we'll know more after the clans meet and vote.

"What are you thinking?"

"Sorry, I spaced out. I'm thinking about the future, about us, and about the situation at Internal Affairs."

He kisses me, sits, and takes my hand. "I can answer some of those questions. The future for us is simple. We are mates. We need to see my pack and let them know you exist and that you belong to me. Some rules could prevent us from living with the pack, but I doubt they'll see you like a challenge. After that, we can make a decision. I will never make it for you. You can be head of Internal Affairs if you want, but at night, you come home to me. That's what most human couples do. We just need to take things one step at a time."

It seems so easy for him. I have to take things one step at a time, but I'm feeling positive about the future. I know I'm not alone anymore, and Jade is part of the pack too.

"You're right, one step at a time. Right now, I want to enjoy my mate. As for Internal Affairs, I'll think about it. I'm not sure yet what I want to do. So, where do we start?"

He pulls me onto his laps. "That's simple, we do what we want. I'm ready to do whatever you want."

I can feel his dick against my side. "My body needs some attention."

His eyes turn bright yellow, every time I say those words, his wolf wants to come out and play. "You are such a tease. He wants attention now." Just as he starts to kiss me, a knock at the door separates us a little.

"Did you hear that?"

He nods his head. "Pretend you didn't hear it."

The knock becomes stronger and louder.

"I'm sorry, mate, but I think we need to open the door."

He groans against my skin, but he lets me go. My legs are shaking with need as I stand and move to the door before opening it a little to see Kane standing there.

"Sorry to disturb you, but we have some visitors that are here the for stone."

"Who?" I ask, as my mate comes behind me.

Kane seems embarrassed. "Two warrior witches are in reception and asking for it and to speak to you."

"Why do they need to see me?"

"I'm not sure, but they wanted to see you before they take the stone to the Librarian."

I nod, but I'm still confused. "I don't understand, but if they want to see me, we'll meet them."

With that, we follow Kane, and he takes us to the room I was in the first time I came here. We enter and see two women—warrior witches, as Kane had said. One seems older compared to the other. Before I have a chance to say anything, the older one speaks.

"I'm sorry we've come without warning, but we need the stone so she stops having problems with her magic."

The younger one seems to be in pain, or maybe it's more that she seems slightly out of control. I look at both of them, I've never seen anything like this. "I'm Casey, I was told you wanted to see me."

"Sorry, where are my manners? I'm Lilandra, and this is Juniper. We are warrior witches. I think you know a little bit about us. We wanted to thank you for retrieving the stone."

I nod.

"Good, she got the call from the stone you retrieved from Damaris. Until she takes it back to the Librarian, she'll have problems with her magic. Not a lot, but enough to make it difficult for her to continue. You have it here? We need it back to put in a secure place."

"You say she's suffering?"

"Not a lot, but enough to understand not to miss the call, and not to give up until she's retrieved it or someone gets hold of it that shouldn't. That will cut the link she has with the stone."

I know warrior witches are on the front line, but I didn't know about this issue until the other day and I feel for them and what they are going through. "Kane," I call.

The door opens, and the half-demon arrives. Lilandra calls to Juniper to stand, and she heads toward Kane.

"Please?" she asks him.

Kane is a half-demon that can rip someone in two, but

against someone asking like this, he has a soft spot. I nod at him. The stone doesn't belong to us. As soon as Juniper grabs it, energy appears inside the room like a thank you and the girl starts to breathe easier.

"We thank you for this. We have enough with our calling and job to do, it's not fun," Lilandra explains.

"I know. Daywalkers are the same with our jobs."

She smiles. "I thought daywalkers were legends."

I laugh, I get that a lot. We are more like ninjas inside the faction, we belong, but at the same time, we're always in the shadows. "We are flesh and blood."

She looks at my mate. "It's weird that we're starting to see this more and more."

"What?" I ask.

"Mating between species. A human has a better chance to be a mate to someone within the same faction, but this is new. We know it's happened in the past but not like this."

"You mean more than just an exception?"

"True, I'm sorry. I didn't mean to disrespect you. We have some individuals that have disappeared, we guess they mated with someone from another faction, or they are gathering things to bring a rebellion to us," she tells me.

Lilandra's body suddenly jolts.

"Did you receive a call?" Juniper asks.

She nods at her. "Yes."

Juniper sighs. "You're just back from one."

"Is it like this all the time?"

Lilandra looks at me. She seems exhausted. "No, but it has been going on for a couple of months now. We know it's not normal but we have no choice but to answer the call. I'm sorry, we will get going, my new mission is waiting for me."

Kane opens the door and shows them the way toward the front desk so they can sign out before they leave.

"What are you thinking?"

"I'm not sure, but the situation isn't normal," I tell my mate.

"You're right, Casey. From the latest report I've had, things are getting worse," Kane replies as he returns.

"What can we do?"

I want to help. Some will die, some will leave. What is the purpose of all this? Who wants a blood rebellion in the community?

"Not much more than we are doing now. We have to stay alert in case we come across something new. More factions are joining us in trying to figure it out. It doesn't only affect one but all of us. It will be the first time in history that everyone is working together for the same goal."

The future will tell us.

*** The End***

Continue in The Seal of Solomon, with Lilandra Reeves's story.

USA TODAY BESTSELLING AUTHOR
NADINE TRAVERS
THE
SEAL
OF
SOLOMON
A LILANDRA REEVES ADVENTURE

BLURBS

Seal of Solomon

Someone wants to control the demon, with the Seal of Solomon. It magically called the witch warrior specialist, Lilandra Reeves.

Lilandra needs to travel to Vancouver, and rescue the Seal of Solomon, but she's tormented by the death of her fated mate, who was killed during a past mission. She throws herself into her work, and faithful servant to her coven.

But when a werewolf named Donovan offers her a chance to bring her mate back to life, in exchange of the Seal, she's forced to choose between love an duty.

Will Lilandra get herself tempting with the promise of a resurrected mate, and will the magical object spark a faction war if she does?

CHAPTER ONE

A Few hours after meeting Casey:

"Luckily for you, we were able to retrieve the stone." I smile at my mentee." Juniper, with everything that has been going on, we have started to notice, the faction, internal affairs, and Supernatural Intelligence Agency have to work together. That's bigger than us."

The agency is right in the Old Port of Montreal zone, almost all the government buildings are in that area, to give access to each species that need it, a way to communicate with them.

"Gwen updated us on the current situation, and we know why everyone has been getting more calls than we used to." We continue to walk, taking the metro.

We start to walk toward Le Plateau-Mont-Royal in Montreal. The land of the witches, covens big or small are all here that includes everyone in the specialty school here as well. A few of us opened a little shop inside the neutral zone, and humans love that little boutique. Since most of us are gone on missions or are devoted to our craft, we, witches, don't have the time to make money in the neutral zone like vampires and werewolves do with their clubs, hotels and everything else they own.

"You think the Librarian is already at the coven?" Juniper asks me. We get out of Sherbrooke Station, and head outside, the weather is gorgeous. We bask in the sunny day because it seems that this year mother nature has decided to take a longer vacation and bring us more humidity and rain.

"I'm sure she is, she knows that she has to pick up this little baby. If she isn't there, and she is busy, then we will call her, but most of the time, she is on time and there, so we have nothing to worry about." The witch's land is right beside the Paranormal University land and the neutral zone. The building on witch land are not tall like they are in the neutral zone or the other factions around it, but what humans see is triplex join, which it is not.

We arrive at the corner of St-Denis Street and Mont-Royal avenue east. We start to walk toward the library on St-Denis street. For a reason, we don't own all the shops in town, some yes, but humans own most. The witch's faction was the only faction that has more humans than witches living within it. The vampire faction has started to allow in more humans since some of them could mate with humans, same with the werewolf or shifter faction.

Entering the big library, we start to head towards the back -- some witches that are working smiles at us. We see a door that says employees only, we push it As soon as it closes, and we identify ourselves, the decor starts to change, and we can see the big command center of the witch's warrior coven.

"It's about time that you arrive, Lilandra. The Librarian is waiting for you in the conference room."

I smile and look at Juniper. "I told you."

Juniper shakes her head. "Yeah you did, I'm going to my place, if you need anything, you come to see me." I nod at her. Usually, the mentor and mentee pairs don't have such a significant gap between them. However, Juniper lost her mother younger than most other warrior witches, and in a way, she feels like I'm a mother figure to her.

On top of that, we have a different calling. I'm a jewelry witch, and she's a stone warrior witch. For sure, they are close, but at the same time, she should have a mentor in the stone witches' warrior.

I enter the conference room. "Ah Lilandra, it's good to see you. I got the call that you retrieved the stone." The Librarian is the one that archives, but also protects objects that don't need to fall into the wrong hands or its not time for them to be back in the world.

"Librarian, good to see you again. I see that you still got your bodyguard." She smirks at me.

"Don't mind him, he wants me to know he is there, but I try to make him invisible." I laugh. I had heard about what happened, and why she got a werewolf for her bodyguard.

"You can't avoid your duty and go for an adventure." She makes a funny face at me. Her small frame resembles a faeries shape. She replaced the old Librarian a few years ago. She's wild with her short brown hair and bright yellow eyes. Her last adventure almost got her killed, which is why the Elder's gave her a bodyguard. Not that the Librarian is in danger, but she's a significant danger to herself. "We are not here to talk about that. Are we?" I could tell that my words had annoyed her.

"Sorry, and yes I agree, you are here for this. The philosopher's stone." I give it to her. Taking it in her hands, her eyes start to light as she gets a good look at it. "Oh, this is the one that gives invisibility to the one who wears it, not only that are commanded by will." She grabbed an ancient cloth and placed it on the stone. Her bodyguard brings a wooden box over which she uses to store the stone. "You got a lot of calls those days?"

"We are all tired, for some reason, a lot of people have been calling, and we don't understand why. Most of us are not in the cover right now, and if we are, we are there only for a day or two." I sigh.

The Librarian passes her hand through her hair. "This is not a normal situation, and you know it, Lilandra. You're the oldest here, and you mentor more and more new witches as the decades go by." Everything she says is the truth since my mate died, I threw myself into my missions like warrior witches, but also keeping up with mentoring any witch that I needed to.

"So I heard that your cousin Megan is at Paranormal University." The Librarian smirks. "Yes, she is, that is what my aunt told my mother. I haven't seen her yet, but I guess with everything that is going on in the community, my path will eventually cross hers." It seems like it had been such a long time since I had been to the Paranormal University. All witches warriors go there for at least two years before they transfer to the coven in the witches' faction.

"I have work to do, Librarian, and I need my sleep before going back." Her eyes widen.

"You already received another call?" I nod at her. She smiles at me apologetically.

"Be well, my friend, and maybe I will see you later." With those words, she turns around with the boy followed by her werewolf bodyguard.

I leave the room only to turn the corner in the corridor to find Juniper. "Mentor, you need your sleep." I take a moment to really look at her, she is young but so talented. She graduated from Paranormal University at the top of her class. All witch warriors have a unique ability, in Juniper's case, she can use her katana and gun with spells, which means she is always ready to fight. She is even one of the best with hand-to-hand combat.

In my case, I'm a little different. I don't have a weapon; my magic makes any weapon that I need. I'm one of the witches that are invisible inside the witch's faction; most of the warrior are noticeable with their weapons. "I know little one. I need to sleep." I jolt a little feeling the call go through me.

"He is persistent?" I smile.

"I know I will take a power nap to get a little sleep, then I will go retrieve it."

She stays beside me. "You know what you have to retrieve?" I nod.

"The Seal of Solomon needs our protection, which is not good." We arrive at my door. All of us have room to rest before heading toward each of our houses. I didn't have one or need one. I have a small apartment, but I tend to not use it a lot, brings back too many painful memories.

"Why do you say its not good?" I open my door, and Juniper follows me inside my small room.

"The Seal of Solomon is a piece of jewelry that can control demons, any kind as per the legend. If it needs protecting, that means that someone is after it to control demons or bring them power. Neither of which is good at all."

Juniper sits on a chair beside my desk. "It's weird that not all of us got the call?"

"From experience, we know that's not normal. We don't have all the puzzle pieces so we can't say what these people want or what their plan is. I know that the Supernatural

Intelligence Agency has all of their division working on it, but also some of the factions and now even Vampire Internal Affairs."

She gets up. "I will let you get some sleep. I guess I will see you when you get back."

I smile at her. "You know how it works. You may get a call for yourself before I get back. Don't worry. We will see each other." She nods and leaves me alone in my room.

Another jolt goes through me. "Virtus summon." I cast, before the darkness claims me, I get another strong shock in my magic. I suspect that my power nap will be shorter than I need.

THE LADY

Inside of the secret society headquarters

"ARE we close to finding the Seal of Solomon?" I ask. I need it.

"Yes, it has been hidden somewhere in Vancouver, BC."

I look at my screen and my assistant. "Why, Vancouver?"

"The Seal of Solomon was brought from Jerusalem for its protection. It's hidden in one of the New Ways Churches, one of the oldest ones." We need that Seal.

"You know that we need it. Those demons don't want to work with us. I will make them do so. That jewelry will come in handy."

The Seal of Solomon is a piece of jewelry that controls demons, meaning I could summon them and also force them to do my bidding. "Which team did you put on this."

She looks down at her paper. "We dispatch Donovan and

her mate, we will also put Jeremy with them. That way, he will focus less on Damaris case."

Jeremy was working on convincing Damaris, the vampire that got taken by that daywalker bitch Casey, to work with us, and join our cause. We got lucky because just after meeting Damaris, he was caught and brought into the Supernatural Intelligence Agency for interrogation and no telling what else. He didn't know much about us, but he knew enough to bring us to the attention of some faction. Since he was taken, we are on the move and our plans have been put on high speed. Jeremy had tried to rescue Damaris when he was transferred to his brother Alto. Fortunately for me, he didn't succeed, for all we know Damaris has already been tortured or worse, is dead.

Alto is the head of the Sutton family, one of the more ancient and powerful vampire families. He mated a human, and because of his blood that flowed through her veins, she gave him a son, Bran which turned Lizbeth into a vampire. She was Damaris first mission and he failed to kill her before she could get to the investigation team. Finding her mate, Kane, a half demon on the way, the mission became muddy very fast. Casey, on the other hand, led the hunt to find and detain Damaris and when she succeeded it compromised all of us. Now because of that most of the factions know that something is coming, but they don't know our plans. Which helps us in our quest or should I say my revenge against the paranormal community that betrayed me.

No one knows it, but they will soon enough. Now is not the time though; I need more power and a magical object is the way to get it. The seal of Solomon is the perfect way to get the soldiers that I need, because they will have no choice but to do as I command. I will crush those who put me in exile, and everyone who is helping me while thinking they are helping themselves.

"My Lady?"

"Yes, Selena, what is it?" I jump back to the present at her words.

"We got news from Donovan, they have located the object, but it's very well protected."

"Since he is a werewolf with a witch as a mate, they are more than capable to handle the situation, sooner rather than later. If they aren't enough, they also have the vampire, that should give them all the help they need."

Sometimes I don't understand why people see some mountain of obstacles that makes them think a mission is not possible instead of just crushing it and succeeding.

"From what I know is that it is hidden in an old part of the church. Not only is it underground, but it is protected by magic."

I look at the news and look at the screen. "What kind of magic?"

"That is what we are trying to figure out. It seems very ancient and so far we haven't found any documentation on it ."

I try to look at it, how it the energy feels. "Did you scan it?"

"Yes, we did, my Lady. It seems that our database doesn't include that kind of magic." I know from the history of the seal that some other species protects it, even demon fail to capture it for themselves. They don't like that an object could control them and would rather kill than be controlled.

"They have traps also, not only witch magic but elf traps."

My assistant looks at me, disbelieve. "What do you mean, faeries?"

"I got some intel about this, but I didn't want to believe it. They gathered old witches in the past, and we don't know when. It seems that one of them has a link with the faeries.

Those traps are so covered in fae signature that I can guarantee it."

"You mean, not only do we have some old witches that created a barrier of some kind, but the faeries put some traps too?"

I knew those traps, never made any, but I have seen them. The light fairy did this, they are the best in that field, add in the power of the earth witches the traps and magic effect of the barrier is probably multiplied.

"I can say those are old. Very old. They have a particular signature, which I think that Donovan could smell and his mate should be able to keep it from going off. For sure, they can do it and not set off the traps. If they do, we will have trouble finding it. Tell Donovan to smell around and try to look for old magic, his wolf will alert him of any danger."

She nods at me and starts to speak to Donovan. If that is the case, this seal will be more challenging to retrieve, which will lead to more time for the witches' warrior to get it instead of us

CHAPTER TWO

LILANDRA

I WAS able to get in a short power nap, but that was the best I could do. I had to go to Vancouver to get the Seal as soon as possible the call I was receiving was getting more urgent.

"Going again?"

"Juniper, you just made me jump. Yes, I am. I was able to get healed and catch a little sleep, but now I have to head to Vancouver. That's the call came from." Juniper sits on my bed. "You didn't receive any call yet?"

She shakes her head. "No, not yet, I need to get back on my feet after the backfire in my magic with the stone. It didn't help me get fresh to start again."

I smile. "Maybe, but you need to rest. You never know when it will be."

She winces at me. "You're not my mother, Lilandra; you're my mentor." I poke her forehead.

"I may be your mentor, but I'm also your friend, and that

backfire in your magic was huge. Enough for you to not be able to fight properly."

Juniper jumps to her feet. "Maybe, but I don't like sitting on the sidelines."

I smile. "Youngster, always going forward. You need to learn to contain yourself. You need to regroup faster in case of another call. Did you forget everything you learned at Paranormal University and with me."

"Stop the lecturing; I know what I'm doing. I..." She jolts right on the spot.

"Well, I guess you got a call sooner than you thought." I grin at her.

"Yeah, I know. Fuck."

I look at her. "What?"

I sigh. "I need to go to Scotland."

"That call is rare, what do you think it is?"

"I can't believe it, but they are going after another stone." Part of our studies was not only learn how to fight, but also how to use our magic with a different kind of weapon. We also learned about our specialty. I have the jewelry specialty, meaning all of the legendary stones and magical objects that are hidden on earth call us when those objects need to be retrieved and taken to the Librarian for safekeeping or protected. We don't understand why, but for some reason they can disappear from the Librarian's vault.

"Which one?"

"The stone of destiny, the one that can help a person on his quest to influence of everyone choice."

"That's no good, if they got both of the magical objects that we've been called to, they could control the demons and influence people to elect the wrong person with that stone too. I think that someone or that organization is starting to get smarter and faster."

I saw that Juniper got another jolt harder than mine.

"Your case is worse than mine." She nods and hugs me. Leaving without uttering another word, I knew she would be on a plane to Scotland very soon, which gives me time to prepare and head toward Vancouver.

Another sharp jolt makes its way through my body.

"I see you got another call." I jump.

"Carl, yes I do, I need to head toward Vancouver, the Seal of Solomon security is jeopardized." Carl is the head of the coven. He has never been a witches warrior or any other type of witch or wizard. One of the only things he could do is the knowledge of people calls, and knowing how to help them on their quest. One of the others is the ability to help us prepare and get our magic up to one-hundred percent, even more in some cases.

"That's situation is going to be very difficult."

I take my bag. "Maybe, but I have no choice in the matter, and you know it."

He pinches his nose. "Maybe, but that's not normal, The situation could become chaotic at some point, which would not be good. I am unable to track all of the summons that we have been getting and some are harder than others. We are not going to be enough to answer this call."

"What do you want me to tell you, Carl?"

"Nothing I guess, but as I said this is not normal. Most of you witch warriors are tired, and you only have a small amount of time to heal and recuperate. Something bad will happen and soon if none of you are at your top."

"I have to go, Carl."

"Fine, Lilandra, I didn't have time to help you with your magic. You will need it more than you know. I need to balance you."

Another jolt shocks its way up my body, even stronger than the last. "No, time for that Carl, I need to jump in my summoning circle and head to Vancouver."

I start to head outside, the way that we travel is with our personal summoning circle, they stay here until we are dead. No one else can see or use them, only us and our fated mates could.

I put my hand on the ground. "Peregrinatione pergrinatione adducere volo me esse." I cast, and my magic circle appears. Jumping in it, I travel directly toward where my call is pulling me.

I appear beside a church, receiving another jolt in my magic letting me know that I was close. I knew that this church was one of the ancient ones in Vancouver. The people who started it came directly from Jerusalem, where the seal came from. Some legends said that some warriors of that time came here to bring a lot of different objects. Some magical while others were more religious. Touching the ground, I know that the seal is under it.

Opening the door, the church was empty probably due to the time of day. It was starting to get late, and most of the people were headed towards their homes.

"Can I help you, the door will be closed soon."

I look at the priest. "Yes, I'm looking for the Seal of Solomon."

The man keeps coming closer to me. I get a feeling that he is not what he is supposed to be. "Why?"

I sigh. "Are you the guard of it?"

"You know too much about this. Speak! What are you?"

Getting up, I know he is not a priest like others could think. "I'm not the enemy here."

He tries to grab me, but I move to fast for him. "You're one of them! The ones who came here earlier today."

Well that is not good, that means that the people I am supposed to keep from getting the Seal are here. "No, I'm here to protect it. It calls to me."

He laughs. "That is not the first time that I have heard

that. The Seal is not only sacred, but it can't fall into the wrong hands. I have sworn to protect it with my life and no one will have it." Removing his tunic, I notice that he is way to built to be a part of the church. He may be a bodyguard or a special guard for the Seal, but there is no way that he pray all day, training yes-praying no.

He leaves me no choice though so I start to cast my spell. His stance lets me know that he is ready to fight to the death, if needs to be. "I don't want to hurt you. If you will just listen to me, we can discuss it. I am not here to fight you, you don't know what is coming."

Smirking at me, I cast a gun and shield. His eyes widen at my weapon. "No magic can touch me." He charges at me, and I slam him with my shield, scorching the shirt on his back.

"I can do more damage if I want, you are attacking the wrong person right now. Do you know what a witch warrior is?"

He flinches a little, but continues his charges. Blocking him again, my spell pushes him hard this time, but he still stays on his feet. "You're not human. I can tell."

He smiles. "I'm immune to magic, it can slow me down, but you're never going to hurt or kill me with it."

I know what he is instantly. I've never fought one of those bastards before, but I know they are hard to kill. "You're a fucking half-giant."

"You did your homework. Now, tell me why you're really here."

"I already told you, the seal called to me. I need to bring it to safety. A clan with a different kind of creature is trying to retrieve it to use against all of us. We don't know all the details yet, but a lot of us are working to find out." I keep my distance from him, I can see him thinking over what I said, but if I don't convince him. He will catch me in only a few minutes or maybe even less.

He was starting to get bigger. "That's what the others told me, that he wanted the best for it. His lies almost cost our priest his life. Now, no one will come close to it. No one." He charges again, this fucker needs to understand. Dodging him, I need a big blast so I can take him down and follow my call.

If the other group has already tried this, it only means that they will try again. I need the Seal and I have to bring it back with me at all costs. Luckily, my teleport circle is close to the church, but without knowing exactly where the seal is it will take me time to search for it. He tries to punch me, but I block him with my magical shield, which pushes him back. " The more you hit it, the more it's going to push you back."

"That's a wicked spell, but it doesn't hurt me."

"It should, but you seem immune to the damaging part, but not the push of it. I'm here to help, not to fight you. I don't want to hurt you and know that your actions are pure. You want to protect this place and anything that is inside."

He snarls at me. "I will until my last breath. You may be able to push me, but that doesn't hurt me at all." Again, he takes his stance, and I need to figure out something. I have read about half-giants, but I have never encountered one. With time, maybe something will spark my memories about something. I just need to knock him down and rush to the seal, grab it, and run to my circle. That way I can be back at the coven as fast as possible.

Looking around, I see a support beam, maybe that could do the trick. It would be a physical attack and not a magic one. Hopefully it would knock him out, but then again I don't know how hard their head is. I start to cast with my other hand, picking up the pieces, which will not make the church collapse.

"Stop Roan!" A male voice yells at him. He stops in the middle of his charge, and I stop casting my spell.

"Why master? She one of them."

"No Roan, she is not. Stop this right now."

I finally take a deep breath; The relief courses through me that the man can control the half-giant. I was starting to run out of options. Turning around, I get a good look at the man, he is short and hunched over giving away his old age. Roan goes to stand beside him.

"It's not good for you to be up."

He smiles at Roan. "Stop being a worry wart, I'm good. Now, you said that you were part of the witch warriors?"

"Yes."

"Prove it."

Grabbing my long black hair, I show him my tattoo. Every witch warrior has to get one. "See Roan. A real witch warrior has the mark. Each of them have it in different places all over their body, but that is how you can tell. Make it glow."

I smile, to humans, it looks like a tattoo, but for those that know us know that it is alive and moves on our skin. Complying with his demand, mine glows, lighting up the darker room and waves. "Come with us. We will talk."

Releasing my warrior magic, I return to normal. Side stepping the half-giant, I can tell he doesn't believe it. "Don't worry. I'm with the good guys."

CHAPTER THREE

Donovan

"Fuck, that was close. That half-giant. I thought they were legends."

I wince, my wound pulling as I look at my mate. "I know love, but now we know that legends could exist, let's just hope the dragon shifter is not here, or it will be bad for us."

She continues to sleep, her healing magic around me. Us, werewolves are strong, but that half-giant is way stronger. I have battled half-demons, which are bad ass but this was worse. "We need that seal. The Lady has to have it. That's our mission."

She gives me a weak smile. "I know love, we can't go back until that artifact is in our hands, but now I'm pretty sure that one of the witch warriors is on his way or is already there. We need to scout around and get more information. You can't do it, during the night, Jeremy will have to do it. The village knows our faces now, but not him, since we attacked during the day."

I snarl at her. "I don't trust that fucker, he may be a vampire, but he was with Damaris, which he didn't succeed in rescuing him. Now, I'm pretty sure that his brother Alto, is having fun with him, if he's not dead."

My mate kisses my lips quickly. "I know, but we have to work with what he has, and for him, he has to carry out this mission to repay his debts to Damaris memories." I give her a look that conveys how unsure I am.

"It could work until he discovers something, we need to be careful with him, we need to keep him in the dark and play with the fact that it was Damaris wish."

Looking at my wounds, I can tell I have a few broken ribs and some internal bleeding. Lucky for me, my mate is a fire witch that can heal. We need this mission to succeed, and remove the factions against us. We have started to find more and more of our mates outside of our faction, which brings more difficulties since the only place that we could be together is the neutral zone, and it's starting to be over-crowded there.

"What are you thinking, love?"

"The big mission, I want to spend my life with you. Not only in the neutral zone but everywhere. I want the pack to see you as one of us." She takes my face between her hands and kisses me. "The neutral zone is not the place to be, and we can't be there all the time. I have a pack to run, and you need to be in your coven. My wolf and I can't go on like this."

She gives me a weak smile. "I know love. I wish some-times that I was human and could fully be your mate, that way we would have no problem with the faction zone."

I take a strand of her hair, red like fire. We are in the wild, and my wolf is close to me, approving of the fact that she is our mate. Werewolves mate for life. Since she was already marked, it was a good thing that most of the witches could not see it and she did not smell like us, but inside of the werewolf faction, most that meet her know that she belongs to me.

"I have never regretted marking you, you belong to us. We will succeed in this, and we will be able to be together for a very long time and have some pups in the process, now is not the time." Sadness show in her eyes, we want to give her everything that we could.

"I know my love, we have to put this aside, but one day we will be able to do so and be at peace, you know that with each revolution we got chaos before the harmony and peace come back. We need to shake those rules that have been intact for centuries."

Kissing her slowly, I know I am not fully healed yet, but I will be before the night is up. "It's right in the middle of the day. We can't do this." I smile at her.

"Us, werewolves, we do it everywhere that we please, and we don't care about the light. I need you, my beautiful mate, we need you. We were close to being separated forever, and I don't want to waste time because of this shyness that you have."

Before she could answer me back, I crush my lips on her. I need her, to feel whole again, to be one with her. My wolf will tell me if somebody gets close to us. Moaning at my kiss, my hand moves everywhere on her body. Her lush curves turning me on as they do all the time. I want it all, to be able to wake up beside her, to watch her belly get round with my child, to live what she should live right now but for those stupid rules, we can't.

"Please." She starts to plead.

"What love? Tell me."

She mewls about it. She can be such a wild cat with others, but she becomes a kitten in my arms. I love everything about her. Starting to play with her big round tits, I began to suck them, slowly like I have all the time in the world. Opening her blouse, I find her zipper and slowly start to work her jeans down.

"Donovan, stop teasing me!" She screams at me. Smiling against her skin, my fingers make their way inside of her underwear and find her pleasure center. Moving her hips against my hand, I can feel how wet she already is for me.

"You're so ready, my love."

"Make me come, my love." She whispers to me.

Starting to kiss her again, I whisper, "Come for me my love, before I reward you with my dick." I crush my lips against her. She places her hand on my bicep, and Her nails cut into my skin. I love this; my wolf is howling inside my head right now.

She moves her head. "DONOVAN!" She screams, squeezing my fingers as she comes. My dick is so hard right now. We need to be inside her. Unbuckling my pants, I push them down, she's on cloud nine right now. Obliterating her pants and panties, she is exposed to me. Legs wide, I can see her pussy glittering with her come.

Opening her legs further, I push my dick inside her, her heat surrounding me. I almost came right there, It's been too long since we were like this.

"More," She asks, my need to satisfy my mate taking over. I have to give her everything that she needs.

I start to move my hips, beginning to find a rhythm to move to begin to the rhythm. She follows my lead, and tightens around me each time I am seated fully inside her. Increasing my tempo, I'm on the verge of coming, but she needs to before I can.

"I'm almost there. Love, I need it."

Both of us are, I want to say, but I kiss her again and increase my pace. I have to possess her, her need to be filled is just as great as my need to satisfy her.

Her sweet inside walls were closing in my dick. They were

like a vise grip. My wolf wants to mark her in the right place, not where it can't be seen. We knew we couldn't right now though, but I need to mark her. To make us come at the same time. Her walls squeeze me harder letting me know that she is right there.

I bite her right under her arm, hard, and increase my tempo inside her.

"Donovan!" She screamed and came. I start to howl as I come with her. Her pussy keeps me inside of her as we try to catch our breath. I kiss her, and she smiles at me. "I love you, my love."

I kiss her tenderly. "We love you so much, my mate."

Now we will wait for night to fall, so that Jeremy can help us. We need that Seal if we ever want to succeed in our mission to have a better life with each other.

CHAPTER FOUR

I FOLLOW THEM INSIDE, the half-giant staying close to me. "You have to excuse him. He doesn't have any gray zone in his thinking."

I smile at the older man. "Don't worry. I have dealt with worse. My name is Lilandra."

"It's nice to meet you Lilandra, I'm Josh. I'm part of this church. If you are wondering, I am human, but since we have more than one magical object to protect. We have many other creatures that live with us. I found Roan and his mother in the woods. Both were in bad shape. His mother didn't survive it. We raised him and took him inside our walls and ever since then he vowed to protect us since he is stronger."

Looking at Roan, he reminds me of Kane that I met at the Supernatural Intelligence Agency, he is a half-demon, but this guy is more prominent, and I could imagine stronger than Kane is.

"That mixte, Is it rare?"

Josh looks at me. "Not anymore, we know that half-demons exists too. Mixte breeds have started to be more common, We have a faction like Montreal does, which I am guessing that is where you came from. The witch warrior coven is existed on in this place." I nod at Josh, he may be human, but he knows a lot about us.

"True, we have started to see more and more mixed race mating these days. We have someone that is trying to hurt us, not only the witches but the whole community. We don't know for sure, but the enemy is old and working on something, the Supernatural Investigation Team are investigating, we have some information but not much at the same time."

He starts to stroke his chin, thinking. "I'm not connected with faction organization here, but this attack tells me that more will come." We enter a big hall, a lot of priests came to us. They are looking at me, with my leather pants and tops with my long trench coat is something that they don't see often.

"Please, come join us. You must be starving. We will eat and talk." I nod and head toward a very long wooden table. Josh sits at the end with Roan sitting on one side while I took the other. I ate when I left the coven, but the fight with Roan has made me hungry.

"You're not a common witch warrior, Lilandra."

"How so?" I look at Josh.

"Usually, your coven has a weapon that they can manipulate with magic; in your case, you cast only magic and it becomes the weapon you need." What he says is true, I just never really think about it much, with all the missions I get I just do what needs to be done.

"I've never really thought much about it, I'm always busy with missions most of the time. Now, it's worse than you can imagine, we barely even have time to rest." This reality is tiring.

"We don't know much here. We have a lot of magical arti-facts. I hope they all do not send a call at the same time, that could be really bad for us. However, I sense something in your energy right now; something bad has happened to you in the past."

I look at Josh. "Are you not supposed to be only human? You're part of a religious belief that was brought about by humans. So what are you?"

He smiles at me. "The church is just a front. We are all partially paranormal. I'm what you call a telepath, which is very common here. Others have small powers similar to mine, but nothing like you have or the other creatures that were here today to steal the Seal. We are lucky that we have Roan because if not, those people would have taken it and left us all dead."

I think about it, and try to remember the information that I have. "When you said half, is that because you're half-human?"

He smiles at me. "No, that means that our power is not strong like most of the ancient paranormal people. We have telepathy but also empaths here, but for some reason we don't understand, we were pulled here like you have been to your faction where you are from. We have witches, were-wolves, and vampire-like those in Montreal, but those fami-lies aren't here for very long. Well, if you compare from Montreal."

In our history books, most of the creatures have arrived in Montreal, most have moved from around the country, which probably why some factions are around other majors cities "You know that if you need help, the agency is there to help. Sure, they are based in Montreal, at the old port, but that doesn't mean they couldn't help." I take the chicken on my plate and start to eat.

"Well, in that case, why are you here? You said you got a call, but we never contacted you,: Roan accuses.

"I told you, Roan, that it doesn't work like that." Josh answered.

I look at Roans eyes; they were light brown, like the earth. "It doesn't work like that for us. Each of the warrior witches have a specialty, in my case I got the jewelry objects, each time that a magical object feels the evil energies too close to them, they make a call to us. We have many different kinds of witch warriors. My mentee Juniper, she has the stone call. Not only do we have to answer, and if we don't, we got a backlash in our magic, not fatal but enough that it could become a danger if we are on a mission. The fact that we got a call like this makes us believe that something is wrong, not with the object, but that someone is trying to find them all. The one thing we don't know is the reason why and who is behind it."

Eating a bite of mashed potatoes, I feel the Seal call again; it's close. "What do you do with those objects, if I may ask," Josh ask.

"That's simple, I bring them back with me, and we call the Librarian in so that she can pick it up."

"The Librarian, who is this person?" Roan asks.

"The work of the Librarian is to retrieve magical objects from the witch warriors when it is not the right time for them to be found and protect them. She's got a very secure place for that." I answer his question.

"And when the time is right for them to be out in the world, what happens to them if they're not at the place that should be?"

I laugh as I get the impression of having my mentee back

with me, when she arrived at the coven, she was so full of questions, that my head spun so fast with her. I smile. "For some reason, we aren't sure why, but when the time is right, and the magical object feels the call to be back and found by the right person, it disappears from the inside of the Librarian's vault. That is how we know that it doesn't need protection anymore. The magical objects have magic, but not like us, the only thing they can do is make a call and teleport back to where they are supposed to be in the first place. When the time is right, the Seal will be back here where you have hidden it and you will not know how it came to be here." Roan seems very curious about all this.

"And who protects the Librarian, you say that it is now a woman, but the last time I heard it was a man." Josh asked.

"True, but his time was up, and his successor was chosen, she's young and adventurous, but now that she has her werewolf bodyguard that helps keep her in place, or well I hope so." Josh chuckles at this.

"She seems very spirited?"

I laugh. "You have no idea. Luckily, her bodyguard just so happened to be her mate, however she doesn't know it yet, but that is the true reason that he is there." Josh got a soft smile.

"For the seal?" Roan looks at Josh and me. "We will give it to you tomorrow morning, you need some rest, and we have a celebration tonight. The Samhain is getting close and we got something to do before this arrived. I hope you will join us for it."

I don't usually celebrate since my mate died, "What happened, my child."

I look at Josh. "What do you mean?" I sit my hands in my lap and look away.

"You were lost in thought, but all of a sudden, you were sad."

I smile at him. "Sorry, it's nothing, life is precious and

time runs slow as hell." I continue to eat. My dead mate is something I don't want to talk about. It is something personal that I like to keep to myself and only release at night when I am alone.

"As you wish, but if you need it. I'm an excellent listener."

I smile. "Thank you, but for now I'm good. What are you doing to celebrate the summer solstice?" I attempt to change the subject.

"It's easy; we celebrate the a good harvest and the fact of the veil getting tinner, and bless everyone. I maybe a telepath, but others are Wiccan inside of this wall. For some reason, I will never understand, but I just love the energy as it's floating around the people. It's recharging, and mostly we still keep those old ways. A lot of humans come for this, every solstice that we have. Which is fun and brings a lot of people around and inside that walls." I could feel the excitement in his voice.

"We need to be careful though; they could be back and try again. Are you sure it is wise to open the doors to the humans?" My concern is not only for the object but them too.

"We have more people coming to help us, and we have Roan, they can't defeat him." I didn't want to say it, but I was positive that the group that came today would do whatever they had to to get their hands on the Seal. Knowing that, I wasn't going anywhere, so I would be here if they needed me. The Seal was coming back with me tomorrow first thing in the morning, and if anything is too dangerous, I will just find it and summon my circle.

We finish our meal, and Josh brings me inside of the place the festivities are happening. "Josh, when you are going to give me the seal?" It's not that I don't want them to celebrate, but I have a mission to finish.

"Soon, Roan will go and fetch it. I know that you're impatient to get back."

"You are right, I am, but I don't want to give them an opportunity to steal it. You know what the Seal can do, right?"

He nods. "Yes, the Seal of Solomon controls demons, which I know for a fact it can do. Meaning whoever possess it will be extremely powerful."

"If you know all of this, them why not just let me go ahead and take it. I respect that it is the summer solstice, but I need to take it with me soon. I know they will try to get it again." I say trying to make them understand my urgency, the Seal needs to be in the hands of the Librarian.

"I know, but now is just not the time. You may have received the call, but I can feel that if you go right now, something bad will catch up to you."

~

Donovan

FINALLY, night fell and Jeremy showed up. "You didn't succeed?" He dares to ask.

"What do you think, they have a half-giant with them, we never expected this. I never thought they really existed."

Jeremy pinches his nose. "So, what is the plan?"

"Tonight, is their celebration of the coming of Samhain, and you need to be there to get close to the temple. You need to enter and find the Seal." Sophia said.

Jeremy looks at me. "So, basically I'm the one that will go in without a safety net and expose himself to everyone." My wound didn't bother me too much, but it was enough to bug me, which leaves my patience running very thin.

"They will know our faces. We made the first move when you were asleep, don't forget about it. We tried to do this without getting you involved. However the warrior witch is here to take it to the Librarian, and if that happens it will be gone until it gets the call for the right person. We can not leave without the Seal. The Lady needs it to succeed at our master plan. We will be around to help, don't worry."

My mate comes around me. "Jeremy, we need you. You know the big picture and why we have to do it. That's also what Damaris wanted." When my mate said Damaris' name, Jeremy shifted uncomfortably, guilt present on his face.

"I know, I'm sorry about all this. I have been having problems dealing with Damaris fate, but I will do it."

I know that we are playing him, and that he will probably not be in the bigger plan, but for now we need the vampires to join us. It was supposed to be Damaris job to make them see, and lucky for us he had been able to convince Jeremy to join, before he got captured, and send word back to his brother. I just hope that he really isn't dead.

"You need to join the celebration, that will be easy since everyone is invited. You need to go inside the church and find the Seal. We know they keep it in some hidden chamber, but you also need to find the witch warrior, she will lead you to it if you can't find it. We need you to be discreet, and we need to bring that seal back at the Lady." I tell Jeremy.

"Fine, I will prepare myself." He starts to leave the room.

"Wait, here take this. This will help you to find the general direction of it. It's like a compass to the seal." My mate gives him something.

"Great, I will use it."

I take my mate in my arms. "Do you think-" I kiss my mate, and make her stop talking.

"Don't talk; he can hear if he wants." She nods at me, and I continue to kiss again.

We need to succeed in our mission, and Jeremy is the key.

CHAPTER FIVE

Lilandra

I was not a happy camper right now, the celebration is going great, but I can't let myself go. I keep looking around or glancing over my shoulder waiting for something to happen, I need to get the Seal and head back to the coven.

Roan is walking and eyeing everyone, I guess I'm not the only one that can't let loose and celebrate. Josh is in his element though, smiling and talking to everyone. I can tell a lot of people are humans, but there are different kinds of paranormals here.

"Relax my friend. Nobody will come here." I look at Josh.

"Not sure, I know those people want it at all cost. The last time we were lucky, a daywalker captured a rogue vampire, who just so happened to be wearing the stone that had been causing my mentee's magic to backlash." Looking at myself, I noticed that I was tall compared to Josh, which was normal with Witch warrior women, I always thought it was because we needed to fight the same way as the men.

"You said a daywalker?" I smile.

"Yes, a daywalker, Casey, and others in the internal affairs of the vampire faction exist."

Josh is surprised. "I thought they were a legend. There are a lot of things that we don't know though."

"More than you even know, Don't worry too much though. We all thought daywalkers were a legend. The cherry on top though will be if the dragon shifters come back. We know that they disappeared for some reason, but we think they are extent."

Josh stroked his chin. "Interesting, we have the book here on a different subject, but I suppose that we don't know all of it. I'm the only telepath here, and humans are the others most of the time." I look at people that were dancing in the street.

"Are each pagan Sabbath and other calendar events celebrated here?"

He looks back at the group of people having fun. "Yes, we do. For most humans, we are a regular church, but most of us know the difference. That serves us, we can grow inside of the human community, and for those who can see them ally with us. You don't have this in Montreal?"

I see that faction exists here, but it's nothing like what we have. I don't know for sure why, but I do know that Vancouver community is smaller when compared to Montreal.

"We have the neutral zone, for those that want to mingle with other species. In the witch faction, our territory is very limited, and mind you, we are closer to humans compared to the vampires. The fact that people are more open to what they call 'a new age philosophy' can stay the way they are and not hide like the vampires. You know that we don't look at humans like they are our next meal."

Josh chuckles. "True, but nonetheless you can't walk around in another factions territory?"

"No, you can pass by it on the major street, but a werewolf can't come to a witch's store and buy something; the same with us, witches, we can't go into the werewolf territory." The more that I talk about it, the more I see the problems in the future. Will we always be able to find our mates inside our factions? I was starting to have doubts about this. A werewolf is the only paranormal who can't control who they mate with. A century ago, we had some humans join different factions due to mating, but now we see different things such as witches with werewolves.

"Did you find your mate?"

I jump at his question. "Did you dig in my brain again?" I have respect for telepaths and their culture, but my thoughts are my own and a space that only belongs to me.

"No, I asked a legitimate question. You're old enough to find one, and by the way, you look so somber sometimes and I can feel the sadness coming off of you, so I was just wondering."

Memories of the past force their way into my head. Some images jump in my memories. Did I have a mate? Lucky yes, but now it's been a decade since he passed on to the other side and left me alone.

TEN YEARS AGO.

I was asleep in my bed, but I could feel someone kissing my skin, that feels like butterflies touching my skin. I smile.

"Ah my love, you're awake." His deep Scottish accent turns me on each time that he wakes me up.

"I'm not sure yet." He continues his exploration. His touches start to be more precise on my body, and my hunger for him increases. Turning around, I look him in his deep blue eyes that stand out paired with his long dark red hair. His tanned skin a stark difference against my pale skin.

"I love seeing you like this every morning." I smile, knowing I look like a mess. My long black blueish hair was all on the pillow.

"Are you sure you are looking at the right person? My hair has to be all over the place." He chuckles and starts to kiss my eyebrows.

"I love your hair like this in the mornings, it means you had an excellent entertaining night with your mate." I slap his shoulder.

"You just think that because of this. I will say it is like this though because someone plays with it during the night."

He kisses my nose; his lips so close to mine. Biting my lip, I crave for his lips to be on mine, to lose myself in him. He is my everything. Crushing his lips on mine, I moan with his touch as he caresses my breasts. Putting my arms around his neck to touch his skin, I want every connection with him I can get.

I have had plenty of lovers in my life, but because of him, I now know the difference between lovers and fated mates.

I met him while I was on a mission in Scotland. In the beginning, I thought that witches warriors couldn't have mates; my life was just too dangerous. However, he refused to let me go, and I couldn't let him go either. When he found out I was a witch, it didn't change his feelings for me. After that mission, he came back with me to Montreal and we lived happily for a decade, until that fatal night.

He followed me everywhere when I was on a mission. We couldn't be apart, human life is fragile, so many people tried to warn me, but I didn't listen. I wasn't careful and that cost me everything. My love, my mate, was gone.

"Hey, are you with me?" Josh, ask me.

Blinking a few times to clear the memories from my head, I say, "Sorry, I was lost in my thoughts."

He smiles at me as a father would smile to his children. "Don't worry. I was wondering what happened that triggered you back into your head." I shake my head.

One thing I don't discuss is my life with and without my fated mate. It's been years since anyone has talked or asked about William. Since I vowed to help the new witches to integrate into the coven, my life was only my missions and supporting the new witches like I was their mothers. My body will always crave him, but I can't be stuck in the past. That only opens up would that were only half closed and would never totally heal.

"Why the sadness?" I look at Josh.

"Sorry, part of my past just showed up and not all of it was bad, but part of it didn't end well."

He put his hand on my arm. "I'm a good listener?"

I give him a weak smile. "Sorry, but no that belongs to me only, and it will always be that way." I start to move; I need to put this in the back of my head and only bring back the best part of it. A light breeze raises, and a chill sweep through my body. Looking around, I can tell something is wrong. Even Josh stops in his tracks, and looks around. The light breeze transforms into a cold one; most of the humans don't feel it; only those that are close to their powers will do.

Josh looks at me, he too felt it. "Vampire."

Why would a vampire be here? I start to search around. "I need to find the vampire." He nods at me.

"I need to find Roan, he may be immune to magic, but not to vampire suggestion or control." On that, Josh leaves me, and I start to walk around. Needing to find the vampire soon, this could end with a blood bath, but I also know that the vampire is here for the Seal. I don't know much about half-giants but when I get back to the coven, I am going to change that quickly.

All those people having fun have no idea what kind of danger they are in. My magic is itching my fingertips. I need to be ready. Anything can happen as I get closer to the intense energy. The vampire was here, but not anymore. All of us who have power, even some humans, some more than others can not only track magical objects, but creatures as well.

It's not my specialty, but I can track some, other witches are specialized with this, they are part of what most human military would call, search and rescue. The energy shift was getting closer to the church -- no sound, which was not good at all. I start to run, and the cold energy is there.

When I feel the Seal leaving the church, time stops, I need to find out where it went. Rushing around the corner, I see Roan, running toward a man, that I don't know.

"Roan, what are you doing?" I ask, but he doesn't stop or acknowledge me, not even when Josh tries to reach him.

I hear him say, "Here master." as he hands him the Seal, my Seal that I need to bring back to the coven. That man doesn't have an aura. As he turns in my direction, I know right then that he is a vampire and has enthralled Roan to give him the Seal.

Josh tries to reason with Roan, but all he does is grab him by the throat and start to shake him.

"Roan," I scream at him. "Stop, you'll hurt him, and you will regret it for the rest of your life." I knew enough to know that Roan felt as though Josh had been a father to him.

He growls at me. "Show yourself, vampire. Don't be a coward and hide behind the half-giant.."

A laugh sounds as the man steps further out of the shadows. "Well, if it's not the witches' warrior. Not only in this past week, did I meet a daywalker, but now the witches' warrior is in my path."

"And you are?" I dare to ask.

"Oh, where are my manners. I'm Jeremy, but you don't have the pleasure of knowing me." His eyes become redder and He knows that controlling the half-giant will take most of his strength.

"Don't try, vampire. We witches are immune to your suggestion."

He smirks. "Maybe you are but not him." I look to my right and see Roan preparing his fighting stance. I know that magic doesn't have any effect on him, but it would be nice if it kept vampires from controlling him as well.

Mihi videtur guns!

With my two guns firmly planted in my hands. "Well, a witch that doesn't have any weapon, it's rare."

A lot of time the paranormal community is surprised that I'm a witches' warrior. "Well, you will see I can fight anyway."

Ultraviolet ammunition!

I see the vampire called Jeremy flinch a little. Yes, a vampire hates anything that has ultraviolet properties.

"Now, we can have some fun." With that, I start charge him casting a sleep spell before he runs after telling Roan to protect him. Not good, that the half-giant is fucking immune to my magic.

Jeremy

HUMANS ARE SO easy to manipulate, I'm about to find where that Seal is inside the church. I know this place was just a front; it was really a temple with different kinds of paranormal creatures and lower species. Usually, the older creatures had their spaces, but others, like some of the empaths, telepath or any kind that doesn't belong in the significant faction are more likely to join together somewhere that others won't reach. Nonetheless, they are human, even if they are enhanced.

When night fell and Donovan told me about their plan and this celebration. I was more than happy to roam the streets that were full of people to gather information. It had been easy to lure those enhanced humans and get more information about the church. They couldn't pinpoint the exact place that the Seal is, but most of them knew father Josh and were happy to tell me about the half-giant that they call Roan who protects them. Donovan, and the enhanced humans told me that the witches warriors was here, oh well more to play with.

I didn't succeed in rescuing Damaris, and I will always be indebted to him. No matter what I will make sure that this revolution happens and that everyone will have the chance to live without those factions.

Getting closer to the church, I am able to spot the half-giant, it was difficult not to see him. I need to find the witch warrior, but she didn't stand out as well as he did.

"Hey, you need to come with us, we are going inside the church and after that we will dance with musicians everywhere when they start to play." I look at the young lady that was speaking to me; it was obvious she didn't know what I was.

"Is it always like this?"

Her happiness was evident. I suspect that she is more than a regular human, I don't know what for sure but I know that other species exist but younger in the timeline. The oldest is, for sure, vampires, werewolves, witches, and fairies. Now we got more, demons and giants always exist, but with time were able to procreate with humans and give them a small portion of ourselves. I suspect, she's something else. "Come."

"Are you inviting me?"

"Yes, I am. Now it's special. You need to loosen up a little, come join all of us."

I smile, usually, we can't enter this kind of place, a real church with religious people inside, we are forbidden to come even if we are invited. In this case, I know this is a front. This is not a real church like the humans create. Thankfully, because I follow that girl that invited me inside. They are so easy to lure, humans believe in everything.

"You're not from around here, are you?" She asks me.

I smile a charming smile. "No, I'm a tourist. Can you tell me more about all this?" As she talks to me, I concentrate all my thoughts on the half-giant. I have never met one, and I wonder if they are easy to control. I need to get closer. Heading toward him, I start to create a control link, he begins to open his mind, and I'm able to see the seal. That beast knows was it is.

Pick the Seal of Solomon; bring it to me.

I continue my chants at him; my mental link with him getting stronger. He starts to move, the priest beside him call his name, but that half-giant doesn't answer. He continues walking; the priest gives up and raises his shoulder starting to talk to someone else

Pick the Seal of Solomon; bring it to me.

I continue my mantra. He gets out of a tunnel a couple of minutes later and starts running toward me.

"Roan, what are you doing?" A woman's voice calls to him. I turn around and she's right behind me,. The half-giant didn't answer, but I knew right then she was that damn witch warrior.

"Roan, bring it to me." The half-giant did as I said.

"Here, master." He told me. I smile and look at the woman again.

"Protect me, my slave," I order him after he gives me the seal.

"Stop him now." The same woman yells again, she has to be the witch warrior. Starting to run as fast as I can, however witches have tools to help them run just as fast. I smile, knowing that I would win today. Another victory towards our end game, just like the Lady told me. We need the Seal and the power that comes with it.

I hear the witch casting a spell and something stung me on the back of my head. She didn't succeed in her sleep spell. I'm too far away from her. Looking again, I see that the half-giant is fighting her now. I don't care that in a few miles my link to him will stop, by then I will be too far away, and I don't care because I will have gotten what I came here for.

I head back toward the camp. We need to leave like now. I'm not going to let the witch have enough time to find us. We will be long gone, with the seal, heading back to Montreal where the lady is waiting on us. Today is a good day, the day that the rebellion is getting stronger.

―――――

CHAPTER SIX

―――――

Lilandra

"Josh, Roan has been enthralled. I need you guys to distract him. I need to chase that vampire." Josh, starts trying to talk to Roan. again

"No Roan, don't do this." I hear Josh's voice. His voice is weak.

Tracker activate!

Targeting that fucking vampire, I see Roan charge at me out of the corner of my eye, but Josh's group was able to stop him. I didn't have the time for this, the vampire was getting further away the longer I stayed here. "Go, Lilandra, we will keep him busy. Take care of the seal." I nod and start running to catch the vampire.

Now wasn't the time to lose him, I don't need backfire in my magic right now. Most of the witches warriors got them when they weren't able to do what they were called to do. Seeing him right in front of me, I cast a push spell on myself to give me more speed.

"Bring it back, bloodsucker," I scream at him as I start to close in on him..

"Forget it, witch. The Seal is mine." I charge him, needing to fight him. Lifting the gun in my hand, I shoot him right in his thigh, a regular bullet wouldn't do anything to a vampire, but the ultraviolet ones do. He starts to slow down before turning around and looking at me.

"You will pay for that." Taking my stance, I give him the sign to bring it on. "You know that with this I could control every demon or beast around here."

"Probably, if you know how to use it, which I doubt."I laugh.

"OK, witch, now we fight." He charges me, and damn those vampires are fast. Luckily he is slower than usual with his wound.

"Are you losing blood, vampire?"

I knew better than to tease a vampire, but he brings out that side me. I need to keep him busy while he bleeds. His wound isn't fatal, but the blood loss from it is, which could make him loose control. His eyes start turning red, he is pissed. Good, this is just how I need him to be. He needs to make a mistake. "You think that I'm alone in all this, you are wrong." The vampire scream at me.

Before I had the chance to do something, someone grabs me from behind and throws me on the ground. Shaking my head, I see a werewolf. Casting for another gun, but with silver bullets this time. I have two different enemies now and I have to be prepared. Aiming at the wolf, I go to take the shot but I am stopped by someone throwing a fire spell at me.

"Watch it, witch. You don't hurt my mate." A female witch says, fire element.

"Why are you against your kind?" I didn't get it, this made no sense.

"You know about fated mates right, I know who you are, Lilandra." That voice, no that's not possible. She gives a signal to the others not to move. "I see that you remember me."

"Sophia? What the heck, the coven said that you were dead." Why had they lied, why was I not told that she had found a mate and rebelled or whatever was going on here.

She laughs. "Well, dear friend, you can see that they are lying, not only to you but to all of us. You know what it's like to have a mate."

That bitch, she knows about my fated mate, she knows everything, she was my best friend. I cried for her when they told me that she was dead.

"Sophia, I can't live without him. I'm empty." Sophia had put her arms around me, as I started to cry on her shoulder. I don't have a lot of friends in my life, being a witches' warrior makes people see you differently, but not Sophia, she was always there for me.

I didn't want to remember, and it hurt that I didn't want to remember. I close that wound and seal it so that I could remain inside the coven, helping younger ones starting in this life. I do my missions, the way I was born too. I never wanted him to die.

"You mated a vampire?"

I laugh, and the werewolf starts groaning beside me. "No, someone more fun than a person that sucks blood to live, a werewolf is the best." Sophia just put herself beside that werewolf, who was still transforming and started running her fingers in through furs. "You remember the pull, the fact that you couldn't think of anything other then him and only him. That is what Donovan is for me. The same as William was for you."

I wince, I know too much about what the pull of the fated mate is. What it is like to be with that mate, how it feels? I miss it every day. Every fucking day of my life.

"You know that I can kill your mate. You know my power." I start walking closer to Donovan, the vampire tensing beside him.

"Don't Lilandra, I do not want you as my enemy, but if you do this, our friendship ends the same as your life."

I chuckle. "You know that I'm stronger than you, you're only an elemental." She winces, and I can tell that I hit my target. In the past, Sophia, wished she was a witch warrior when we were at the Paranormal University, she always told me about it. As soon as we started school, I knew that she couldn't be a witch warrior. She was like her mother, attracted to the fire.

"Trying to hit an old wound, I see what you are doing and it won't work. I have to ask do you miss him, really miss him, or have you put a forget spell on yourself to forget, to be empty and alone in your life."

It was my turn to wince, she hit her target. "I think talking is getting us nowhere. I will ask one last time because we used to be best friends. Now, hand me the seal, and you will be breathing for the next century with your mate." Sophia looks at her mate. I know that mating a werewolf brings something different as they can communicate through thought. "What is your decision, Sophia?"

Without replying, her mate charges me and she starts to cast a spell to help him. Shooting a silver bullet at them both, I miss my target she has always been good with fire, but I can tell she has learned a few new tricks.

I start to cast an earthquake under their feet, needing them out of the way so that I can get to the vampire who has the Seal. They both jump before he starts running towards me again, with her casting a spell as he runs. Backflipping away from them, I get closer to the fucking vampire.

"Sleep." I cast trying to slow them down. Hitting the werewolf with it, but since that kind of spell was not my specialty the effect wasn't the strongest. Running toward the vampire in front of me, I begin to shoot him with the ultraviolet bullets causing him to hiss.

"Give me that Seal, vampire."

"Never, you will have to take it from me. I advise you to forget about it. I'm very old and of true vampire blood. I can fight you. The ultraviolet bullets will slow me down, but not kill me."

That fucker, a born vampire, what he says is true my bullets will only slow him down. It's not rare, but it's getting harder and harder for vampires to have children with their real mates.

"Give me the seal."

He takes it from his pocket and shows me. The calling is getting stronger the closer it is to me. "This is what you want. No, I'm not giving it to you, it belongs to us. It will help us, and that way, I can fulfill my friend's dream. A community without borders..."

"Shut up, Jeremy. She will not understand. You know where to go, we will distract her. Bring the seal to the Lady."

"Lady?"

Donovan, the werewolf, looks at me. "You will not understand. You were supposed to have died alongside your fated mate, if he was actually yours. I am starting to doubt it though."

It may have been a decade, but I can't contain my hurt and anger because of his words. "I may not be able to kill him, but I can you , and that includes your fucking mate, Sophia."

Sophia jumps at my word. She has never seen me this way. I start to cast a regroup spell for anything in my energy range to become a weapon with silver material. "You will pay for this." I fill my energy with my hurt and not my anger. Magic that comes from anger is hard to control. Everything with magic has consequences, and need balance. Using my anger could turn me into a black arts which a witches' warrior and I don't want or need that in my life.

My fingers tingle, and my eyes become white. That is when my power is at its strongest. I can make weapons with magic, any kind, and sometimes it could turn ugly.

"We need to go, love. That's her strongest spell." Sophia did a wall of fire and stopped most of the weapon that I had made. He howls and starts running with his mate, Sophia. I turned around, and the vampire was gone. I need to find him. It needs to be at the coven with the Librarian to be protected. It is too much power for them, and I know that it is going to be bad news for us-terrible news.

Concentrating on my tracking device, I follow his mark, I have no choice but to get the Seal back. I need to stop that fucking vampire, fast.

CHAPTER SEVEN

The Lady

"We got new from the team, apparently a witch warrior is against them. But Donovan got only the time to text me to said that Jeremy got the seal."

I smiles at Selena. "Good, very good. Jeremy could run very fast."

Selena phone buzz. "Oh, but that witch it's Lilandra Reeves."

I looks at my paper, I got all information on some kind of possible people that could go against us. I found it. "The witch warrior that lost his mate ten years ago."

"What are you thinking?"

I need to make her join us. She will be a great addition to our team. She's one the most powerful witch warrior that exist. She could summon different kind of weapon at her choose. She doesn't carry weapon like the other does, her magic make it at will.

I see a side note from Sophia, I start to think. "Selena, text Donovan back. I got something that Lilandra Reeves couldn't resist that for sure."

I start to write on a paper, my casting spell start to work. My assistant looks at what I'm doing not to sure but after I finish my last letter drawing, she looks at me disbelieve. "You can do this my Lady?"

To be a black faeries got some advantage which bring some part of the craft that other will never go there been afraid of the price. I can pay it, I got not issue with it.

"Text him, and tell him about this but he need to make Sophia the deal, she was her best friend before."

She nods at me and I start to see her finger one her phone screen. "It's done. I really hope you can do it if she's accept it."

"Don't worry my dear Selena, I'm able too and I want her to join us. She need just a little push and that gift it's something that she could never wish or have in her entire life."

Her phone buzz again. "Donovan said that he relay the information to Sophia, and they are talking."

I looks outside, she will make a very good addition at the team that for sure. I got everything in my power to corrumpt a witch warrior and not only that she's one of the best that exist.

Sophia

"Sophia, read this."

I take Donovan phone as I watch Lilandra chasing Jeremy. "She's serious?"

"Yes, I ask a double confirmation about all this. I don't know if she can, but I guess she want Lilandra to be part of us and that's her ultimate gift to join and be whole again."

I looks at my mate. I doubt that the Lady can do something like this. I'm disbelieve to be honest. "Do it, I follow you. I transform and jump on my back we will chase after her." He strip of his close and I jump on him, been an alpha is the fact that he is not only strong but big also.

After a few minutes to running around, Donovan catch they smell and follow it. I could see that Lilandra stops Jeremy in his course. She got so different kind of weapon against him, some ultraviolet one which we know that will only slow him down.

"You're bloodsuck, give me back that seal. It doesn't belong to you." She points some of her weapon direct at him.

"You will not be fast enough to shoot."

She chuckles at Jeremy. "Don't tell me bloodsucker. My reflex are after than my thought and my magic is trigger with my reflex."

"Stop Lilandra. I got something for you."

She make other guns appears points at us. "Don't got any closer. You're a witch but you betray your coven with him." I looks at my wolf mate, he didn't change, but he is on his guard. We are all against her.

"I got a deal for you."

She snorth. "Really, a deal. Since when you cut deal, Sophia?"

Donovan nods at me. "I got a message from the Lady."

"Lady? Who is she?"

"We don't know much just that she's trying to put the faction together so that way we can be one. No more bound-eries. You know what that means."

She looks at me. "That's what you're looking for. You're delusional, Sophia. Those faction are there for something to protect all of us."

My anger got better than me. "What do you think you will do if your fated mate is with a different species. You got lucky, yours was human. But human are weak and know that. That's why your got kill at the end."

Her eyes start to come more blueish than usual. My

temper got better of me but I need something far away from Jeremy. I got something that she want, crave for a decade.

"You know nothing about losing your mate, Sophia. You were supppose to be my friend and all the sudden you disapear only to reapparea with him. Everyone in your coven thought you were dead, and that include me." She didn't move but some weapon got closer of Jeremy.

"Lilandra, I know that you're empty without him. You think that your job and your mentee could fill that whole inside you. It will never."

"I make something with my life and love my mentee. They are my family. You were part of it at some point in my life. Now we are enemy, Sophia." That I know but I got a wild card in my hand right now. I start to approach her with my mate beside me.

She start to shoot at my feet. I know that she will not kill but that trigger Donovan to snarl at her. All his teeth showing her not to mess with us. I need to calm down the game right now. I don't want a bloodsheed before I'm able to make the deal with her. In a way I wish that my best friend was with us, but if I got to choose she will be second every time, Donovan is my mate and he is my priority.

I can see that Jeremy want to take advantage at the fact that Lilandra is concentrate on us, but I shake my end negatively, I know better from her. She got eyes around her.

"I don't want to be your enemy, my friend. You was always my best friend and you still are."

She chuckles. "Really? Well, your action doesn't match your mouth."

She start to create more weapon I know by fact that she not kill me, and if she does, she will kill Donovan in the same time. She maybe against us but she value fated mates.

I continue to walk toward her, but she put a gun at my head. I make movement so that Donovan doesn't do anything rash. "I'm telling you, Lilandra. I got something that you want and we can give it to you."

I can see in here eyes she doesn't believe me.

"You got nothing that I want, only that seal, which I doubts you will give me freely."

I make a pause, I need to watch my temper and my tongue. I'm a fire witches, we got reputation to be hot temper.

"Lilandra, please. Remove that gun. I got something that you want. So much. That you will be happy again, like before."

She looks at me septical.

"I'm listening."

She don't remove her gun on my head.

"Talk."

"It's rough to talk with a gun at my head right now."

She remove it but put it in front of me. Donovan, got closer of me. I know that if I do something wrong, both of them will fight until blood will be shed.

"Now!"

"The Lady, she very powerful that she told us. That she could bring your dead fated mate alive if you join us."

Lilandra

I lost in my track my focus shift. "Impossible." Nobody can do that, expecially they don't have any real body anymore. I put him in the fire myself.

"Please love, wake up!" I scream, my eyes are blurry with my tears. I don't want to believe I didn't want to acknowledge it. "You can't leave me alone like this. Please, love. Wake up for me." I start to hit him on his lifeless chest. His body was cold. I can't believe because of those fucking missions, and the fact that he didn't want to wait for

me but be all the time with me. I put him in danger. I'm the one that is responsible in all this.

"Lilandra, you need to burry him. He is dead, Lilandra." I turn around. I know that voice, Sophia my best friend.

"Leave me, I want to follow."

"No you don't you need to find that ring. You need to avenge him but claiming back that ring." I want to kill someone, I want to hit someone. I'm not that type of witch but right now I don't care. The fated gave me my mate, and now it's claiming back. Why on Earth did I do to have this, but leave this. That emptyness inside me, my heart stop beating when his stop too.

"Sophia cast fire and burn him. I will be back here but burn him. He never want to be burrow inside underground. Please, Sophia, do this for me."

Sorrow, emptyness, all kind of emotion fill me. That ring is gone, the call stop. How I can track it again. "You're sure?"

"Please, Sophia, I never ask for anything in my life. You're my best friend. I don't want to face the coven yet, but I need him to be free."

She nods at me, and she cast it. I kiss his cold lips and I remove himself. The fire hit his body which it's start to burn, I let go of my tears. I will never see him again, only the memories, our memories will stay. I know she cast her biggest spell to cruch everything magicaly and she shatter the bone in the same time. I keep his ring in my hand.

I look at him. We were fated mate, life bring us together. I know in my heart that no one will replace him, but for him that was important to have a human wedding, for him that ring belong to his mother, that's the last thing that I have of him. All my picture and memories will stay but that will not heat up my bed at night or our apartment. I will need to be relocate because I will never be able to stay in the place. That place belong to him, and we make something special about it. It will only bring me the pain, the lost and the emptiness in my heart.

I look at Sophia, I know how much magic energy that she need to bring this kind of level of fire and cruch. She smiles at me. "I want to be alone. Thank you my best friend."

That day I wonder around, without any goal. My life is empty now, only thing that exist is those mission and be a mentor, like the coven ask me. Nothing will replace him, that part of this past belong to me, and me alone. That's my fault and the only way to make him proud of me is to serve the coven like I should have and I should have put him in the apartment and make him the sleeping spell. But how could have, I love him so much that I want him to be with me all the time. I want to be one with him.

That night came back like a flash. "Sophia, that's impossible. Even a necromancer can't. I burn him for a reason. I didn't want to have the possibility of bring him back."

That night, that was my reason, if I didn't ask her to burn him, I may have reach someone to bring him back.

"No, I'm telling you. If she said that she can, she can. You have to believe me."

"I need that seal. I need to finish that mission." It's been my only focus with my mentee for the last decade since his death. I vows at the coven to be the best mentor that they have. That became my life line for all those years. That's how I can continue with my life.

"Don't be stubborn, Lilandra. You know how it hurt that day. I know why you ask me to burn him and to cruch his remain. I know why."

"So you know that impossible to bring someone back, if we don't have to body to bring him back. That's impossible, and if someone can, it will not be him, that's not possible." Sophia got closer. That pain is back, inside of me, that hole that never heal it's was just put aside and I try to fill with something else that could never replace him.

She put her hand on my shoulder. "Lilandra, listen to me. I'm telling you if she said she can, she could. That I can guarantee it, the same way you ask me to put his body in hash because you knew that I could do the job properly."

I looks at her, but for a reason I could see him clearly. Juniper never was able to summon him, she never was able to know if he was close. She's not only a witch warrior but also a clairvoyance by her human mother. If she can, that mean that is not wondering on earth which it's impossible for anyone to bring him. I can see Jeremy, for a reason he didn't flee. I need that seal I need to make him release Roan from his enthrallment. I make a pose, but all this need were mine, that doesn't belong to me, only for other. What are mine needs?

CHAPTER EIGHT

Sophia

I focus all my thought on Lilandra. I know that she's lonely, she hide it but she need to face right now. She need to ask something for herself, no one will give it to her, only the Lady could.

I could see her emotion in her eyes. I know her since kindergarden, we got separe way because she's a witch warrior and I was part of the fire coven. That's how we got separate after Paranormal University was finish for her.

"Lilandra think, no one never did something, to give you your dream, your life that you should have with him."

Donovan got close of me. I know he fell my emotion right now, his wolf is very connect with me. I need to make Lilandra see, to make choose us. "The Lady can, Lilandra. Join us, come with us. You will have everything that you want, your mate back in your life, and alive. You could have a future with him."

"That's impossible, Sophia. The body doesn't exist anymore. You need that. Why do you think I ask you to do what you did. For this, so that no one could lure me in that kind of deal. I didn't for him, so that his spirit is free, that he can move on."

Lilandra chuckles cynically. "Really, Sophia. Since when you care about me. After that day it was never been the same between us. Never got close. You finish with that dog and betray your coven on top of that. That's what you think when you join the coven of fire?. That's the life that you want. A traitor. Someone that will put his want first. We got mission, even you got some. Don't tell me they never ask you to be part of some."

I want to hit her. I'm powerful and I know it. My casting is the best it is in the fire coven. I'm on top of all. "That doesn't suit you, Lilandra. You're not that type of person that will hit with word. You're are more physical than that."

"What guarantee do I have?" She maybe doesn't want to believe but in the same time, I know that she miss him grately.

"None, only my word."

"Which is almost nothing. You're a traitor in the witches community and you know it."

"Watch it, witch warrior. She maybe could do nothing but that's not my case. I will not let you talk to her like this. Never."

Donovan charge Lilandra. I try to stop him without success. I know that I'm a traitor but my mate because my priority number one.

Lilandra

Part of me want to fight that urge to ask about this. I lower my guard but as soon that Donovan charge me because I didn't be polite with his mate. That put my guard up again.

"No, Donovan. Stop. I can defend myself." Sophia try to

make reason with him. No dog got reason, they only feel what they wolf feel.

Clypeus

With that shield I'm able to hit Donovan. My sadness give me all the energy that I need to fight him. I can see out of the corner of my eyes. Jeremy is still there, and without notice it, he start to get closer of me. He got the seal and I need to put him uncounscious so that will remove the enthrall to Roan.

I push Donovan and start to run fast toward Jeremy. He didn't see my coming. I maybe sad, but no one will promess something like this. No one will tempted someone with anything they want.

I hit him, hard with all my magic that I could my eyes start to blurb, I know I do what it's the best for the community, for everyone. I know that part of Sophia word are truth. I never ask anything for me, not since that fatal day. I know that my great mentor, told me about this could happen, but I was thinking that I was above all this, that's could happen to someone else, but not at the great Lilandra.

I start to fuel with all those emotions that I hide inside me. To forgot that hurt, that pain. No I start to fuel at it, to help me achieve what I should achive.

I transform my magic at a baseball bat, full of magic and I hit Jeremy with all my strenght and magic, all. I didn't want to kill him, it's harder to kill a pure blood vampire.

"Watch out, Jeremy." She scream at him. To late, I hit and he fall down on the grown, I pick up that seal. I look at it. I cast the embed spell to hide it in my skin. That will remain here until I'm back.

Before I got the chance to start to run again, Donovan push me on the ground and with is fang out he start to growl at me. He try to put my arm side by side but before Sophia could get closer I cast two big stone and crush him in between them. I need to get going my teleport circle is very far and I need to make sure that Roan and Josh are fine.

"No, Donovan."

I know that emotion, the emotion that you see that your mate could be dead. I know he is not dead but he will got a major headach and more. I hit him very strong with those magical stone.

"You don't want that gift. You're not worthy to be part of our group. You will never love or been love anymore. You will dead alone and I will watch it and get on your deathbed and tell you how wonderful my life was with my mate. You will pay for this."

She start to cast her strongest spell I know her all my life I know how she cast the same she know that I could fight dirty. "You hurt my mate, Lilandra."

"He will survive, Sophia. You let me go and you will be able to attend at his wound." I try to her think of him and forgot about me and the seal.

"Why Lilandra do you want that gift the Lady want to give you."

I looks at her, I could see she split her magic, one side the fire and the other the healing spell for her mate. I understand why she want to protect him. I was in the same place of her decade ago, but I know how arrogant I was at that time. That wasn't a good period for me, even that bring me my fated mate.

"I can't let my daughter go."

"Your daughter. You never got one."

"You're right, but Juniper is a daughter through my eyes, I can't let that go. She's the reason why I do what I have to do."

I know she will not understand. Juniper is my spirit

daughter I couldn't never let her go. She's why I'm what I'm the better person now to compare before. She's the one that make my laugh again, to see thing with the sun around, and not be part of the raining day all the time. Yes I did my mission, yes I fulfill what it was suppose to be but I was an empty shell she fill that void in my heart and in my soul.

"You will not understand, Sophia. You got your mate but a child even I didn't bear him myself doesn't mean I can't have that spiritual connect with her, you know what I mean."

She looks at me. "You means, for her, that Juniper you will let go everything. You will be alone for the rest of your life?"

"No, I'm not alone, Juniper is there, the other mentee also. The coven is there too help me. We are a family, which you spit on it and that you betray all of this."

She fire me fireball, I know they couldn't go through my shield. "I always think that you was the one that could understand me. I understand you that time, you ask me something and I did it, without question. Now, I want that seal back again."

"No, never. Sophia, you were a friend in the past. I may have hit harder on your mate, but he is not dead. From now, we are enemy. Tell you're Lady that we will find her, and when we did, that will not be pretty to all of you. Don't forget about this. Not only for you, but for all of you."

I didn't want to linger there, I want to be back fast. She didn't cast fire anymore, I can see all her magical energy are at his mate. That I can understand, but the rest I can't. Now I need to be back. I need to make that seal out of reach of anyone that could use wrongly.

～

THE LADY

Somewhere downtown of Montreal.

"My Lady, we got news."

"It's about time, so what happen?" I looks at Selena. "What?" I urge her to talk. She close her eyes and looks at me.

"I'm sorry."

"What do you mean, sorry?"

"They..."

"What?" I'm losing my patience right now. "You tell me right now!" I yield at her.

"I'm sorry my Lady but they didn't they fail, and Lilandra didn't accept your gift at all."

I turns around to see the city. "That bitch think she better than me. Where is Donovan and his group?"

She text something on her phone. "I got Sophia, Donovan is out of commission right now. She hit them very hard. I suspect she didn't want her friend to have the same faith that her. She let Donovan and the group live but she treath them, and us."

"Us?"

Selena take a deep breath. "Yes."

"What she said."

I can see she didn't want to tell me. "She said that she will find you and the rest of us and we will have to paid for our act. She will bring us down."

I take a glass that was on my desk and smash it on the wall. "Really, she treath us. She think that she could bring us down. She doesn't know me, and us. She will paid for that. No one never send me treath about this. They will all paid. We will succeed in our mission."

Selena smiles at me. "Yes my Lady, we will. The cause is a good one. All freedom to us, to choose with who we want to mate and be able to mingle in the territories of other faction."

I didn't said anything, Selena nods at me and leave my

office. Yeah, they will have more. My main goal is not that mission, my real thing is to make all of them to paid with what they did to me. Those faction will paid. They could be involve in all this, but the faeries will paid more. That make me like this, they ban me.

I was beautiful once, but that curse will have to stop. I will kill them each and one of them that ban me, they will paid and they will remember what they did. Their jealous toward me, make them did what they do.

I sit behind my computer and send a message at Donovan. The seal is lost but we were able to influence some demon of the lower class. We need more that seal should give me the power to influence the strongest in they group. With that seal I could have a big a very strong army working with me. A demon is very hard to kill. Now we will to adjust all this, we need to find other magical object to help us or more to help me. I need it all, I need them to follow me without question and to do mission after mission and to gather the more that we can.

That it's my goal, my motivation in all this. I send a private message. I need her help, and I know she will do everything for me. She's been my eyes all those time, but I need more of her, I need to be close of me. Together, we can do all and we could get that revenge that even her wants.

I smiles at that, the plan is to divides the Supernatural Intelligence Agency and all those faction to a merry chase, and after we will be able to hit where it's hurt and they will never see us coming. That plan is brilliant. I need her science and magical expertise, we need to push at the other level.

I smiles at this encrypted message that I send her. Now we wait. I need another object I know which I need. Donovan will have to pick it up for me. He better succeed it. He is the best but since that Damaris fail and put us on the spot light, it's didn't help us to make everything behind everyone back.

My computer shime, I receive the message. Yes, we that will start. I smiles as I read. Now phase two is starting.

CHAPTER NINE

I leave and head back at the church I need to see if Roan got back to normal. I embed the seal on my skin and cast the running spell.

"You're back." I hear the old and deep Josh voice. I turns around and see him. "Yes, how is Roan?"

"Lucky that stop but he is ashame with what happen. We know that wasn't in is control." I nods at Josh. "True, half-giant could be enthrall the same like human does. Where he is?"

Josh start to walk and make a sign to follow him. I enter back in the church and we start to walk toward some old stairs. I looks up and I see that Josh start his climb it. I follow him, after minutes, I can see that we are going at the top of the church. He start to open a window and climb on the roof there. I continue which I suspect he bringing me to Roan.

I'm able to see him, his face on his knee and he look up in the sky. It's not the full moon yet but we getting close of it. "I'm sorry." If before he present himself to me like a big, badass half-giant now I can see it like a children that did something.

"Roan I bring Lilandra back."

I genuily smile at him. "Hey, it's not your fault."

He hide behind his knee. "Yes, it is I'm not strong enough."

I sighs and sit beside him. I put my hand on his back. "Roan, I know vampire. I'm a witch and I got spell to immune myself against that. Even me could be enthrall by them if I'm not prepare. The only species that can't be are demon. They will make you do thing that usually you never do. I hit him to remove that enthrall and bring you back to normal." He looks at me little.

"Maybe, but I will be weak because of that."

"No, Roan, we never thought you're weak even me could be enthrall." Josh sit at the other side of Roan.

"Easy for you to said, you where the one that was put in this. I didn't want to hurt any one. I can't stay here. People will see me the half-giant that go not control over him."

"Roan!" Josh order him.

"Listen at Josh, Roan. That could happen to everyone. We were lucky that we were able to remove that. That could be more dangerous if that keep his enthrall on a long time which that could became permanent." I want him to understand that happen to everyone. Yes, he is a lot more stronger but that he can do his job to protect everyone in the church.

"I will teach you Roan, I never thought you could be affect it. I will give you trick to learn so that you will be able to be more prepare next time if something like this happen in the future." Josh reassure him.

"Yes I want to learn. I don't have magic but I could hit them on the head so that way they can't start to looks in my eyes to manipulate me."

I chuckles at this. "Not all vampire are bad either. The

same in all different species. You just need to learn and prepare yourself. You know that you could be affect by it and you will be more prepare next time."

I give him a friendly pat on the shoulder and get up. All of us, start to going down at the ground level of the church. I need to go back at the coven that seal need to be protect and the Librarian need to hide it.

"I guess that mean you are leaving?" Josh ask.

"Yes, my mission is done the seal got rescue now I will protect it and the Librarian will have to pick it up. When the time come, the seal will find a way to be back and to fulfill what it's suppose to with the right person."

Josh nods and Roan give me a big hugs. He almost crush me. I shake my hand with Josh and I head back at my teleport circle close of the church. I look around, that small place was fun the visit. I will be back one day, I hope too.

Lanuae Magicae

The light surround me and the image of the church became a blurb and I start to see the city again, the witch faction. I got teleport right behind the little new age cafe that witches own and I enter by the back door. I open a hidden door and start to take the stairs down. That were all the community is, the underground is our home, those shop, cafe or any other small business place, that belong at the witches faction, it's an entrance in the real community. The sealing match the weather outside, which give people what to expect outside.

I start to head back at the witches warrior coven, in the middle of the town. I enter the building. It's seems very old, I don't know how long we are living underground but we love it here. We got everything that magic could bring us. Each different coven are there too.

"Oh, Lilandra you're back!" The receptionist welcome me.

"Yes, I will need the Librarian, right now. I got something for her."

She nods at me. "I will do that. We will tell you when she's arrives." I nods and head up in the building. A lot of people is working here. The church at Vancouver was small and more private, here it's seem more big. We're back the business. The mission is a success. I enter the elevator and the door close after me. I have to bring my report in all this. We need to contact a lot of people. They will probably want to stealth other object. We got to be prepare, all of us.

Donovan

Damn that hurt. "Easy, love. It will be better soon."

"Where is Lilandra and the seal?" She didn't want to look at me. I grab her chin and make her looks at me.

"Love?"

She open her eyes and looks at me. I could see the hurt in her eyes. "What happen after she hit me?"

"She could have kill you. She didn't, I know she value the mate bond. She didn't accept. I reach the Lady to tell her the new, she wasn't happy at all. She refuse to have her mate back because of that Juniper girl."

I stroke her cheek, tear is pouring, I could see that she been crying for a long time, some were already try with the dirt.

"That's ok, love. What the Lady said?"

"You could have been kill and all you worry is that Lady?" Her motion got her, I could see in he eyes right now. "Easy, love. Breath in and out. Slowly. Your emotion are too raw and all over the place."

She start to do what I tell her, her healing magic get more

stronger to help me. She focus on my healing but werewolf could heal very fast. "Were are we and the other are where?"

"Jeremy is hiding in the ground, is waiting the night fall to be back with us. The rest of the team got call back at the Lady headquarter, saying that she need them for another mission. For us, I discuss with her or rather Selena state that we have to wait nightfall for Jeremy and you need to heal. Now it's the morning, we got all day. I rent a small hotel room and we can crash here all day. Jeremy know where are we."

I lay back on the bed. I'm better, not hundred pourcent that was sure. But none the less. "What was that gift you the Lady want to give her?"

"Simple, when I talk to Selena before, I told her about Lilandra and how she lost her mate. Selena text me back with all the information that I need to convince Lilandra to join us, her reward should have been her mate, but she refuse only said that she was happy with the coven her mentee and in specialy that Juniper girl?"

"Well, what do you think of her, did you meet her before?"

She shake her head. "No, I never. Lilandra and I became very distant since she got the mentee, I never knew that reason why. I suspect, since she didn't have her mate anymore and got no kids with, Juniper replace that hole she got in her heart. I suspect for Lilandra, Juniper is a daughter that she never got." I looks at me mate, she continue to heal me. I could see that her magic energy is low.

"Stop love, you need your energy back for you. Are you hurt?"

"No, she didn't touch me. She knew that if she but you out of commission that I will but all my magic to you for your healing process. What she didn't do for his when it was the time."

I start to think. "Maybe in a way, even she linger for him,

she didn't want him back since she did wrong to helping him."

I start to kiss her dirty hand. She smiles. "You maybe right. I'm not sure. I know that their couple were a little bit different of what I'm use to see. I don't know which kind of pact they vows at each other."

One thing that fated mate does it's to vows something between them. For me and Sophia that's simple we stay with each other no matter what. That's why my life except for some occassion was in the neutral zone, the same for Sophia. Now everyone know about us and her coven will cut the ties with her.

"How do you feel about the witches community, knowing for each other?"

She give me a fast kiss. "None the matter anymore. You're my priority in life and those mission to have the life that we want and how it should have been and how it will be. I hate that people couldn't love someone that is not in their paranormal species. You can do nothing when you meet your fated mate."

One thing that I love about her, it's her passion. Been a fire element that become more explosive with all the emotion. I know that she love me, all her soul and body the same for me. No one could replace her.

"I know, love." I kiss her knuckles. "We will succeed. We got he Lady and her group and our rebellion start to get bigger since a lot of people want to join us. They are in the same position then us."

She start to stroke my chest. My wound are heal, I smirks at her. "You got something in her head?"

She grins. "Well, I start to wonder what to do to make the time pass. We got the way nightfall before we can move."

Her lazy finger start to have a pattern and she got closer

of my pleasure center. I hiss. "Well, love. You are to far dress to compare of my self."

"I didn't have choice to put you naked to heal you."

She raise up and start to remove the t-shirt over her body and her jeans. She didn't have any undies and bra. Which put my dick harder that he was. "Your wolf got you tongue?" She tease me.

She gorgeous with her long curly red hair. She seem far more sophisticate to compare of myself. But I don't care she belong to me. All of her will have me for the rest of our life. I grab her hand and I start to kiss her, hard. I want to brand her, to make the rest of the world know that she belong to me. She giggles.

"I love your, Sophia, my mate."

I didn't leave her the chance to replies. I want her to show me with her body. Which she response very quickly. We make love all day and we leave when Jeremy join us.

Lilandra

"I see you bring it back." I turn around. They advice me the Librarian is coming after the retrieves call that we make.

"Happy to see you again, Librarian. I see that he follow you." She make a disgust face. "Don't mind him."

I reveal that seal, the jewelery is very beautiful. "Yes, you're right, so beautiful."

"Oh, I didn't notice that I speak out loud."

She chuckles. "That happen, don't worry, and know I can't read mind. I leave that to my cousin."

I give her the seal, and she put it in a small woodden box. "Do you know why they want that seal?"

I sighs. "I'm not totally sure, but according to my research. That seal could control demon, all of them. I'm guessing that Lady start to be impatiant. We retreive some magical artifact that she want and that put a stop or at least a slow down at her plan or project. I guess she want a rebellion, I need to speak with Casey about all this. We need more information."

The Librarian nods at me. "I know that the Paranormal University got their hand full right now." I frond my eyesbrows. "What do you means?"

"You don't know?"

I nods negativitly at her question.

"I got news from one of my cousin. The one that could be a telepath and an empath in the same time. She's there right now. Well she arrives a couple of weeks ago. They got a demon that chase and kill magic people. The university call the Special Operations Team to help them."

"Wow, I hear something is happening at the Paranormal University but I didn't know what was that bad. The Supernatural Intelligence Agency are split in all this. We got the special ops at the university and we got some witches warrior making more mission."

"Not only that Investigation Team also is on that and some major faction too."

"Do you think that got any relation in all this?"

I start to think. "Maybe, but until we know everything, the only thing that we know for sure is that Lady is someone or more than one that are planning and she got henchmen that are working with her. But do you think that the same group that is giving problems at the university and that's why she wanted the seal to control more demon?"

I looks at the box. "Possibly, but we need everyone to help out in this. Something coming and it's big. We need to be prepare."

The Librarian nods at me. "Yes, and that's why I'm need in the field and not in that dusty and dirty suppose office." I hear someone snarl in the back. "I see." I wants the laugh, that werewolf which is put to be his bodyguard doesn't seem to approve. What I know she tries and that's why she got him, which I start to think it's more than it seems.

"All of us need to be ready. I will let you with that seal and we will see each other very soon."

On that I left the room, I want to have time for me in my room. Juniper is not there and I'm fine with this. I need to quiet time before it's hit the call again.

CHAPTER TEN

Lilandra

I'm in my apartment, the one that I have with my mate was rent. At that time I was in need to have a fresh start. I prepare myself a hot bath, I need to take a small break. We don't know what will come and I suspect that will come faster that we are ready for.

I put myself inside the bath and go inside the water, I'm not a water element, but I could feel his energy starting to replenish me. To be a witch that use only his magic energy to create weapon to help my mission, it took a lot but I could regenerated through any kind of element.

I got out and start to dry my hair. I looks at myself. It was tempted that offer. I didn't want to think much of that. I take my pj's and hit on my bed. I lay there, looking at the celling. It's more than a decade that happen, I thought that everything was hidden inside me, which I suspect not. I looks outside, Halloween Eve's is in couple of days, I hope that Juniper is fine with all this.

She never want the other to know about her mother gift.

It is usual and that possibly the only witches to have that kind of gift. Usually, she inside her room that night. Celestia help her with all this, but now I know she's in a mission that could complicate thing.

I close my eyes and put small amount of spell to help me fall asleep fast I didn't want to think of him. I didn't want to relive it. I need my sleep but that will be without interruption.

Lilandra!

I start to walk around, I'm in the darkness right now.

Lilandra!

That call again, but that's not a magical object. "Love please wake up!" That voice, that rich and with a broad accent, I know that voice, I know who it is. It's been a decade without any contact from the afterlife.

"Lilandra, love. It is time."

I want to talk but I seems without that possibility. "You will see me again, soon that I promise."

On that I wake up, I sit on my bed and I'm breathless. Why now? It is because of that suppose gift I know that impossible to bring someone to life without the body and been that long since it's been dead.

An electric shock pass inside me, another call. I got the image.

"No, that's impossible. It was lost."

That image again and again in my head. That ring, that fucking ring that cost my mate life it's back and call me again to save it.

Why now? It's calling say that someone wrong us it and she want to be find. Could have a relation with my dream. That the fact that my dead mate told me that we will see each other because that's why he refer too.

A chance to finish what I wasn't able to finish it. I really wish that Juniper was there. Another jolt inside me, and the word of Scotland appear inside my head. That where Juniper head with her mission the last time that we talk and I know she didn't come back.

Not even in three days it will be Halloween. That ring is been use, but wrongly and want it out. I really got no choice.

I need to fill that mission and succeed it. For Juniper, for my mate and for my salvation. I needs that ring, and I need it now. That the only way that I will put my mate at peace and maybe after that I will be able to contact him if he want it. I hope we could forget me, I hope that I could go back ten years ago, make the thing different, to change my decision and his. That's impossible, we can't return in time, the same way we can't bring back dead people not without a price and I didn't want to paid it.

The balance in the magic is the key, and it's always ask for something. My whole body shake, that jolt again. It's really want me to find it. I will succeed, I will put my life on stake for that and I will win.

I prepare myself. I take an old picture frame; I hide it under my bed. Most of them where destroy but I could for this one. I touch it and sadness wash over me. After that day, I never cry and I will not start now. After, all this is finish I may let myself go in sorrow but until then that's impossible. My priority is that ring and I need to stealth it.

I touch the picture again; some memories came alive inside my head. The way he smell, his touch and his kiss. The fact that was perfect inside his arm, those I don't have since that time.

I leave the picture on my bed. I head out, I need to cast that teleport ring and I need to focus on that ring. One way of the other, I will have it and those who got it will died because without that call my mate will be alive.

*** THE END ***

The adventure continues in Stone of Destiny. I hope you like it :)

ALSO BY NADINE TRAVERS

Urban Fantasy

Supertunatural Intelligence Agency

Vampire on the run

Blood Rebellion

A Lilandra Reeves Adventure

Seal of Solomon

Juniper Samoni Trilogy

The Stone of Destiny

The Stone of Thunder (2022)

Romance

The Mercenaries Series

Renegade

Hacker (February 22 2021)

Sensei (Coming Soon)

ABOUT THE AUTHOR

Dear readers, I hope you love the story. You can follow me here.

**Website: http://www.nadinetravers.com
Series website: https://www.
supernaturalintelligenceagency.com
Facebook: https://www.
facebook.com/NadineTraversWriter/
Twitter: https://twitter.com/NadineWriter
Goodreads: https://www.
goodreads.com/nadinetravers**

Enjoyed this book? You can make a big difference

Reviews are the most powerful tool in my arsenal when it comes to getting attention for my books. Much as I'd like to, I don't have the financial muscle of a New York publisher. I can't take-out full-page ads in the newspaper or put posters on the subway.
(Not yet, anyway)
But I do have something much more powerful and effective than that, and it's something that those publishers would kill to get their hands on.
A committed and loyal bunch of readers.
Honest reviews of my books help bring them to the attention of other readers.

If you've enjoyed this book, I would be very grateful if you could spend just five minutes leaving
a review (it can be as short as you like) of the books on any platform you download it.
Thank you very much.

Newsletter: https://www.subscribepage.com/ntforfb

Nadine 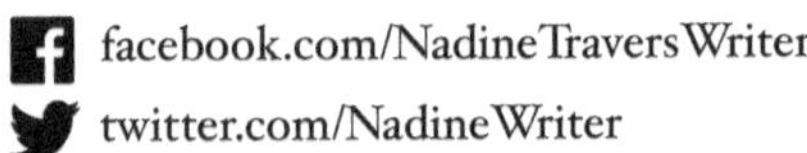

facebook.com/NadineTraversWriter
twitter.com/NadineWriter

www.ingramcontent.com/pod-product-compliance
Lightning Source LLC
La Vergne TN
LVHW042355190726
843493LV00005B/1035